An Ever After Summer

Wishing Springs, Texas—Summer 1870

***An Ever After Summer** is a historical of Matt McConnell's ancestors on his father's side. You can read this before Matt's story comes out. Also, **A Cowboy For Katie** is his mother's ancestors story…love from all those years ago will help Matt in his love story **Heart Healing Cowboy**.*

Mathew McConnell needs help with his baby so he's sent for a mail order bride. All he needs is someone to love his baby, *he's* fine. He'll never lose love again, or trust that God has him in His thoughts. His baby has no mother and a father who has to work really hard to keep the ranch going. So, a mail order bride is his only resource and he made it clear in his ad that he needs a practical woman to keep house and be a mother to his two-year old baby girl—Bible believers need not apply—and he means it.

Ellie has had a rough life, and her aunt has told her she has to be a mail order bride. Ellie looks at it as a gift, her opportunity to make her dream of finding love real. Until she meets Matthew she had no idea the handsome heart throb—didn't want a "Bible thumper—what's wrong with being a "Bible thumper" anyway?

She's lived a tough life and been accused of being a born killer, killing three before the age of one, so being a Bible thumper isn't so bad. Now, she's determined to show him she's tougher than she looks—and just the girl he needs.

AN EVER AFTER SUMMER

A National Readers Choice Award Winner

A Gotta Have Hope, Book Five

DEBRA CLOPTON

AN EVER AFTER SUMMER

Copyright © 2024 Debra Clopton Parks

This book is a work of fiction. Names and characters are of the author's imagination or are used fictitiously. Any resemblance to an actual person, living or dead, is entirely coincidental.

No part of this publication may be reproduced, distributed or transmitted in any form or by any means, including photocopying, recording, or other electronic or mechanical methods, without the prior written permission of the publisher, except in the case of brief quotations embodied in critical reviews and certain other noncommercial uses permitted by copyright law. For permission requests, please contact the author through her website: www.debraclopton.com.

PROLOGUE

Widowed rancher looking for practical woman to keep house and be a mother to his two year old baby girl—Bible believers need not apply. Mathew McConnell, Wishing Springs, Texas

Sitting at his desk in the office of *The Hitching Post Mail Order Bride Catalogue* Melvin Hitchcock scowled at the letter.

"The man is wasting his time *and* money," Melvin grumbled, shaking his head. The ad had been in the catalogue for weeks with no response—other than a few letters from candidates of ill repute who Melvin *quickly* disqualified, after all there was a child's welfare at stake!

Melvin knew something had to be done or the

widower would lose patience and blame the lack of response on the catalogue and not renew the ad.

It was time for action.

Melvin picked up his pen. Tapping it on his chin he thoughtfully studied the letter…a widower. Mathew McConnell was *obviously* still grieving the loss of his wife these two years and not in his right mind. Why else would he forgo the qualification that any loving father would want for his children? No, this *lonely, grieving* widower needed love as much as his baby needed it…and from a woman with God on her side if she were to be of any help at all.

Intent on his task, Melvin tweaked a sentence, removed a few words—only a slight change but enough. Pushing his spectacles onto the bridge of his nose from where they'd slipped he read the new add. "Yes, yes, this will do nicely." It had a certain ring to it. A certain *romance* that would speak softly to a woman of a tender heart and a Godly belief…

There would be responses now. And Melvin trusted the good Lord would show him exactly the right young woman's letter to forward on to Mathew McConnell—

that baby needed a mother and already it had been far, far too long.

Anticipation filled Melvin, helping lonely couples was a calling. He had a way with words, and an inexplicable ability to read a letter and know what someone really needed.

Oh yes he did indeed. It was a God given ability and Melvin Hitchcock had no qualms admitting as much and plans to let such a gift go to waste…

Bible believers need not apply—ha! Indeed they should and they would or his name wasn't Melvin Hitchcock of the very well received *Hitching Post Mail Order Bride Catalogue!*

CHAPTER ONE

Wishing Springs, Texas—Summer 1870

A born killer. Melvina Eldora Smith killed three people before the age of one— Her mother at birth, her father of a broken heart and her poor, poor uncle Mutt outside a bar with a runaway buggy...

Ellie Smith fought off the chanting taunts of her past. Taunts that had followed her from *the ill-fated day of her birth* —as Aunt Millicent was fond of saying.

Three deaths before the age of one!

Aunt Millicent had assured Ellie and everyone else she came in contact with for the last nineteen years that all three deaths were most *unquestionably* Ellie's doing.

Oh how Ellie wished she'd known them all. The

loss of her mother and father especially left a gnawing hole in her heart. But according to Aunt Millicent it was nothing compared to the one in her own especially with the hardship of raising Ellie dropped straight away into her lap. Over and over Ellie had heard this from as far back as she could remember.

The taunts of children on the playground and whispers of adults carried the same message. *"Murderin' Melvina."* The hurtful nickname had clung to her all these nineteen years. Her penance for crimes committed…

But not any longer.

Today, she'd left Murderin Melvina behind, shortened Eldora to Ellie. Her new beginning as Ellie Smith was under way. Today, her very own fairy tale began… She still could not believe it was possible.

Her chest felt like it would surely burst with anticipation as she stood on the weathered plank sidewalk beside the stagecoach she'd just ridden three hundred rough, dusty miles into Wishing Springs. Even the oppressive summer heat couldn't stifle her exhilaration as she surveyed the bustling little Texas town that was now her home. She loved the assortment of clapboard buildings, some made of logs and some of bricks that were a backdrop for the busy people moving in all directions. The mercantile was across the street and the hotel was too. The livery sat at the end of the street. She took the rest in but instead of focusing on the buildings she studied the people. Fingers of excitement curled inside of her, tickling her so that she thought she might laugh with the thrill of it all.

Where was he?

At nineteen Ellie was leaving her regrettable past—and Aunt Millicent—behind and daring to forge a new life. From the moment she'd stepped onto that stage she'd been in control of her destiny—well she and God, but surely He had orchestrated this opportunity and was in on the plan.

Yes, God was finally smiling on Ellie. Good things were about to happe—

"Look out below!"

The shout from above had Ellie looking up just in time to see her heavy valise sail from atop the stage straight at her! Ellie jumped out of the way, barely in the nick of time, and the valise whizzed past her and thudded to the boardwalk in a plume of dust. Ellie's hat slid forward and she righted it with one hand as she clutched her Bible to her racing heart.

"Oops, sorry about that little lady," the grizzled driver shouted.

"That's quite alright, Mr. Muldoon," Ellie assured him. He and his shotgun had gotten her through some rough country without mishap so for that she was thankful. Sneezing when a loose feather from her hat tickled her nose, she swiped it out of the way and continued to scan the men milling about.

Where was he?

Two months ago Ellie had only dreamed of a different life. One with a husband and children to call her own—her unattainable happily-ever-after. But dreams were all she'd had. No man in Fort Worth with half a mind wanted to be stuck with a wife known as Murderin' Melvina. Then Aunt Millicent had slapped a copy of *The Hitching Post Mail-Order Bride Catalogue* in front of her and given Ellie an hour to pick a husband or she would pick one for her.

Looking down in shock at that catalogue, Ellie had no idea that the book would change her life. Hesitantly, she'd opened the book to a random page and as if beckoning her gaze to fall upon it there was Mathew McConnell's ad. The short, sweet words in the ad spoke to her heart.

Lonely, widowed rancher looking for love and a godly mother for his sweet, two-year-old baby girl who needs gentle arms to hold her.

Ellie had connected instantly—not even knowing what Mathew McConnell looked like. She'd looked her future in the face and decided right then and there to change the course of her life.

The very daring of the idea had energized her like nothing else ever had, like being freed from shackles!

And the most ironic thing of all: it had been Aunt Millicent's desire to be rid of her that had turned Ellie's life in this exciting new direction.

It just went to show a person that God, in His timing could take a bad situation and turn it for good...Just like the Good Book promised.

Mathew McConnell was the hope of her life.

The answer to her prayers. Her very own knight in shining armor.

Mathew offered her a way out of the life she'd been doomed to live and for that she would forever be grateful.

And baby Sophie...oh the sweet angel, just like Ellie, had lost her mother at birth. Ellie had so much love just bursting to be showered on Sophie. The sweet, innocent child would never, ever carry the burden of her mother's death as Ellie had for her own.

Searching the passing people, Ellie's eyes jerked to a halt as they latched onto the dark, penetrating eyes of a tall, lean cowboy with a very unbecoming scowl on his ruggedly, handsome face— "Goodness," she gasped, her fingers tightening on her Bible.

Dressed in dark britches, a gray, long sleeved shirt tucked in at his narrow hips, a holster hung low on his right thigh. His thumb was looped beneath the leather belt just in front of the pearl handle of the holstered gun. Tall, lean and dangerous.

And he was watching her.

Ellie wondered if he knew that he looked like he'd just eaten a very sour pickle. And how sad because it didn't become him in the least.

And why, she wanted to know was he looking at *her* with that pickle faced expression?

Hiking her chin, Ellie met the cowboy's insolent stare. How dare he! Of all the rude— He took a step her direction! Ellie gasped and despite the road separating them she took a step back on the platform. When he stomped from the plank sidewalk and strode toward her across that rutted road Ellie's heart dropped straight to her toes. What was he doing?

Sidestepping horses and buggies he crossed the busy street, taking purposeful strides toward her. Tightening her grip on the Bible she clutched to her chest she denied the dreaded thought sliding over her— surely to goodness this man was *not* Mathew McConnell!

Why else would a perfect stranger be approaching me?

Her head was full of imaginations of the way she

believed her betrothed would look. And while, at the moment, she couldn't disregard this man's dark, good looks that scowl that hadn't left his expression left much, *much* to be desired. Ellie was looking for a lonely widower looking for love...he should be looking happily at her.

This rugged cowboy looked like he was aching for a fight or at the least had a belly full of green plums. Ellie glanced about her, maybe her eyes were deceiving her and his gaze was locked onto someone standing behind her.

"Miss. Smith?"

Ellie's stomach curdled, her palms damped. "Yes." *Dear Lord, please don't let this be so.*

"Miss *Melvina Eldora* Smith?"

The name alone caused Ellie to cringe. Aunt Millicent always said a formal letter required a formal name and Ellie had written the letter to *The Hitching Post* in the most formal way, wanting to make the best impression of her life—and with aunt looking over her shoulder! Clearly a misconception on her part, since this dour, pickled-faced man obviously had no interested in making any kind of good impression on the likes of her.

Pulling her shoulders back, Ellie pushed her alarmed reaction down. "Mr. McConnell?" *Please, oh please let it not be so...* The quick nod of his dark head shot any glimmer of hope straight onto the dusty boards upon which she stood. Surely there was something amiss here. Some terrible, dreadful mistake.

* * *

The dread that had been coiling in the pit of Mathew McConnell's gut from the moment the wide-eyed beauty stepped from the stagecoach tightened as she slowly nodded her feather-topped head.

"I'm afraid there's been a mistake," he nearly growled, eyeing the Bible in her hands before looking straight at her.

Eyes that were mingled shades of light and dark blues, like the colors of the bluebonnets that grew all over Texas, met his, just a perfectly sculpted eyebrow snapped up. "Ex*cuse* me?" she said, none too happily.

Mathew should have tipped his hat to the lady, even if he was too angry to think of the manners his mother—may she rest in peace—had taught him. This was not the Melvina Eldora he'd pictured would be arriving to marry him—the woman who'd come to be the mother to Sophie.

"I specifically requested a *practical* woman." Snatching his Stetson from his head, he slapped it against his thigh. What kind of mail-order bride catalogue was this *Hitching Post* anyway? There could have been no mistaking his ad: *Widowed rancher looking for practical woman to keep house and be a mother to his baby girl—Bible believers need not apply.* And yet, here stood this, this *woman*...decked out in her feathers, ruffles and lace from the top of her head to the tips of her dainty boots.

"Practical," she ground out. Her pert nose twitched just the slightest, and her bluebonnet eyes flared with indignation. "You're saying I'm not *practical*?" Her voice rose on the last word as she glared at him and batted a feather out of her face.

"That's right." He'd started this so he might as well finish it. "And I *specifically* said Bible thumpers need not apply." His gaze fell to the Bible gripped in her white knuckled hands.

"Bible *thumper?*" Her eyes narrowed. "How *dare* you?"

"Well, don't get all riled up," he drawled. "You *are* holding that Bible like it's your last best friend in all the world."

Her mouth formed a perfect pink O and a tiny gasp escaped. "Yes. Well," she stammered. "Mister McConnell, I'm not certain what's going on here but you are not the only one disturbed at the moment. You might be angry that a so-called Bible thumper has gotten off that stage. However, I can assure you that the sour-face greeting me after a long and arduous stage coach ride is quite a disappointment to me. A *very* large disappointment indeed," she huffed, pulled her shoulders back and stood rigidly in place, staring up at him with the gumption of twenty frontier women.

Looking into those blazing eyes, Matthew was startled by the depth of emotion he saw dancing there—beautiful, unwavering eyes that held a mixture of ire—and *hurt?* A pang of regret hit Mathew and he found himself lost in that gaze and the emotions swirling just beneath the surface…

And he totally and completely lost his train of thought.

CHAPTER TWO

The insolent cowboy's words stung, though he surely had no idea how right he'd been. Her Bible had been Ellie's first and *last* best friend in all of the world. If she clutched it to her heart it was because, unlike all the other words spoken to her throughout her life, God's words were the ones that had never hurt her.

God's words had taught her at a very early age to shield her heart, and doing so kept the cutting taunts of others from wounding her.

A part of her was glad to see Mathew struggle after hearing her reprimand. It gave her hope that he wasn't completely the ogre she'd feared he might be. But where could they go from here. This wouldn't do. She had to find good in this.

"I came here on good faith after reading your *lovely* worded ad," she said at last, extending him a chance to redeem himself.

His brows wrinkled. Eyes, deep and dark as a midnight sky, flared. "Whoa," he said, as if halting a team of horses. "Did you say *lovely* words?"

She nodded. They had been lovely.

"I never said anything lovely. All I said was I was a widower looking for a practical woman to care for my baby. Bible believers need not apply."

The last words were enunciated as if Ellie were hard of hearing and might need to read his lips to understand them! She understood alright—clearly the man had problems. He was trying her patience no end... She crossed her arms tightly in front of her, fighting exasperation. She was about to do some enunciating of her own—and then his words sank in!

"Wait," she said, flinging her hand up. "That's what your ad said? That's *all* your ad said? And it said practical woman, not godly woman?"

He scowled. "Taking that ad out in that overrated catalogue was supposed to fix my problems." Raking his hand through his hair, he looked flustered, frustrated and...

Cute.

Well that was a positive. She could handle cute much more handily than tall, dark and scowling. That fit more with what she envisioned when she'd packed her bags and stepped inside that stagecoach bound for her future.

Problem was, *she* wasn't what he'd envisioned either.

* * *

"This is that *Hitching Post* fellas fault," Mathew muttered, rubbing the back of his neck, very aware that Miss. Smith watched. "He did something to my ad or mixed it up with someone else's. Had to'of. There was no misunderstanding my ad."

"If that's what you wrote it was definitely clear." Melvina bit her lip. "It was similar to what I read though. Just different."

"Why did I let myself get talked into this," he

muttered. He had a good mind to put Melvina Eldora Smith right back on that stagecoach and send her on her frilly little way. And the skeptical way she was looking at him and biting her lip told him she was likely thinking the same exact thing.

But what about Sophie? What was he going to do with her?

A man didn't like admitting he was desperate, but Mathew was as desperate as he could get. He slapped his hat on his thigh. He had a ranch to keep up with. His ranch hand Lem did all he could, but he was getting up in years, and lately Matthew wondered if Lem was up to the job. Some of his cattle had gone missing and he needed to hire more help. On top of that, he had an active two-year-old running poor old Lem's wife, Maggie ragged. Maggie had been a lifesaver after Beth died, but her arthritis had her so stove up some she could barely get her joints to moving some days. She was struggling.

And with no other close neighbors, he'd let her talk him into this mail-order bride catalog idea.

Trying to figure out his next move he spun, staring

hard at his wagon sitting a few feet away. He didn't want some woman coming in here who would have any inclination to tell him how good God was. He'd once believed that it was true. Not anymore.

"Um, where is Sophie?" Melvina asked, cutting into his runaway thoughts.

He almost broke his neck turning back around. "Sophie?"

"Your child. Or did I misunderstand that too?"

Her eyes held his, her delicate chin lifted. Any hurt that he'd glimpsed before had disappeared behind a cool controlled surface. Like a rock dropping deep in a pond, after the ripple had gone, leaving no trace that it had been there on the still waters. Almost as if she'd put on a shield.

"No, Sophie is real. She's with a neighbor."

The mask fell away and a smile danced upon her lips as the cool eyes warmed like sunshine.

Instant awareness shot straight through Mathew. His heart nearly hit him in the chin it reacted to those sun-kissed eyes. *What is going on?*

She tilted her head slightly, feathers waving. "If

you can find your tongue," she said with a lilt of humor in her voice, "maybe I should meet Sophie. Maybe *she* won't instantly take such a dislike to me."

* * *

Ellie hustled after the disgruntled cowboy who was making his way toward a buckboard a few yards down the street. Her oversized petticoats were heavy against her legs as she tried to hurry. Aunt Millicent had insisted she wear them. She despised the cumbersome clothes! Why did society demand such things? This was the frontier for goodness' sake. She hoped soon she could be free from the proprieties that stifled her—that she could be free to be herself as she'd been the all too few times she'd escaped to old mister Clute's farm. Thoughts of the rough-edged rancher who'd been the one true bright spot of her life snuck up on Ellie, fortifying her resolve as Mathew tossed her traveling trunk onto the buckboard then grabbed her valise and tossed it on board without so much as a word. The man was as prickly as a cactus!

Ellie fastened her thoughts on seeing Sophie and determined that once she saw the sweet child then she'd decide what she was going to do. Aunt Millicent hadn't said anything about her coming home if things didn't work out. No, her aunt hadn't been able to get her out of the house fast enough. So where did that leave Ellie?

It leaves you with the option of having for once chosen your own destiny! Or your own doom. She was going to keep trusting God and she was not, not, *not* going to give up on Him on the first sign of trouble.

"So is the neighbor far," she asked, hurrying close behind Mathew as he headed toward the front of the buckboard. He turned suddenly and she plowed right into him. Staggering back, her toe caught on her skirt and she pitched sideways. In an instant Mathew's hand, wrapped around her arm, strong and steady. He held her upright.

"Are you alright?" he asked, sounding for the first time gentle. His voice was rich and smooth, when not irritated. Her skin tingled at his touch.

"I'm…" Ellie lost her words, catching a flicker of warmth that flared in the depths of his deep molasses eyes. Ellie's insides melted like butter and her breath locked in her throat. Mathew McConnell affected her in the most astonishing way. "I'm fine," she managed. "I'm clumsy sometimes."

Nodding, he released her as quickly as he'd grabbed her. "It's not far."

Fumbling with her skirt, Ellie reached for the seat rail. Mathew's hand once again cupped her elbow. He assisted her as she maneuvered the step and climbed up to the bench seat of the buckboard.

"Thank you," she said, but he was already striding around the front of the horses.

He climbed up beside her and took the reins. Her stomach fluttered at his nearness. "Is your ranch far?"

"About three miles."

"Oh that's perfect. I lived in town in Fort Worth and always longed for the wide-open spaces," she said, fighting to settle her nerves.

Mathew just looked straight ahead.

The man wasn't high on talk. She fought the uneasey feeling that Mathew might send her packing. And much of that had to do with her Bible. How could a Bible make that much of a difference in the way the man looked at a woman? She'd never imagined that the Good Book that gave her so much peace could be the cause of her losing her chance at a new life.

Surely God had not sent her here to be turned away.

Mathew had called her "frilly." He didn't even know her. He had no idea the life she'd lived or the grit that filled her bloodstream. She would not have survived without that unshakeable determination. No, he had judged her without knowing her at all. As had everyone else in her life—other than Mister Clute. It was maddening.

"Does Sophie talk yet?" she asked, seeking to find common ground. He didn't speak for a long heavy moment. Ellie held fast to her positive attitude, and plastered a pleasant smile to her face.

"A few words," he said at last. "And she excels at walking, which is not always good since she tends to try and run like a deer."

Relieved, Ellie chuckled at the image. "I love it. We are going to have a wonderful time." She could hardly wait to see her...her baby girl.

Her own child. Closing her eyes Ellie savored the dream. Opening them, she caught Mathew staring at her, though he instantly looked away, scowling once more.

Yes, as prickly as a cactus!

"It is a beautiful day for a new start." Ellie gave him a wide smile.

Despite things not being as she'd dreamed them, God was good and she refused to think anything else. She would not worry, she would not worry.

She *would not* worry.

CHAPTER THREE

Mathew tried to concentrate on driving. Melvina had been nothing but helpful, which he found irritating, and she seemed totally unconcerned with the fact she was nothing like the woman he'd hoped to marry, chattering and grinning like they were on a Sunday afternoon drive.

His gut twisted. Reminding him of happier times. Reminding him of Beth. Of the pain.

Mathew hardened his heart to the smiling, hopeful beauty beside him. What was he going to do?

He had to work. His daughter needed someone to care for her. Melvina had been the only response to his ad in months—and maybe that was only because of some mistake with his ad. The problem was he didn't have time to wait for a practical wife. Besides the inept proprietor of the catalogue could mess up again! That would be about his luck.

"So, when is the wedding?" Ellie asked, her big eyes as bright as the sunshine beating down on them.

"The *wedding*?" he wheezed. "But you haven't seen Sophie yet."

"I don't have to see her to know what I want. Despite getting off on the wrong foot with you, I want to be Sophie's mother," she said, her eyes imploring. "I've been sitting here thinking and I know I'm not what you were expecting."

She'd been chattering away—how could that be thinking? *He* couldn't even think with all her chattering.

Placing her hand on his forearm, she set his pulse immediately into a gallop. "I fell in love with your daughter the moment I read about her."

The truthfulness of her desire rang in the earnestness of her voice.

"I came to be the mother of your child. I've made a commitment to that. I promise that I can be what you are looking for. And, I don't know what you have against frills and Bibles, but all of my clothes don't have ruffles, I promise. And I only brought this *one* hat."

What a relief—the thing was atrocious.

"That aside," she said without a pause, "I promise you, if you give me a chance I will do everything in my power be a good and loving wife and to be a loving mother to Sophie."

Her hand on his arm tightened and her eyes grew soft with longing—Mathew thought his heart was gonna bust out of his chest and beat the horses to Maggie and Lem's place.

Sophie—this was about his motherless child, he reminded himself, tearing his gaze from Melvina's intriguing eyes.

He struggled to focus on what was best for Sophie, fighting to ignored how Melvina's touch was causing him all kinds of problems. He'd fought anything and everything that had come his way—the war, Indians, frontier conditions...bears even outlaws. He'd survived it all. Surely he could survive a thumper.

Melvina hadn't backed down from the commitment she'd made to his child.

Despite not wanting to, he admired her for it.

Could he do no less for the commitment he'd made to her?

Truth was, so far she hadn't quoted scripture like he'd expected when he saw her clutching that worn Bible. She'd pulled her hand from his arm and now sat waiting for his answer.

"I planned on you meeting Sophie and then if all was agreeable with you, we could swing by Reverend Jacobs after leaving Maggie's and make it official." Originally, he hadn't wanted to waste any time getting the hitching done. He hadn't wanted to give either of them time to change their minds. He needed this plan in action. He had cattle that needed tending, and a daughter who needed the same.

But looking into those huge eyes, his stomach felt queasy. This suddenly seem rushed. "...*Or* you can have a few days if you need it," he added quickly when she didn't say anything. "Maggie would be fine with you staying with them for a little while."

"No," Melvina said, relief radiating in her voice. "I think your plan is *perfect. Just perfect.*"

He frowned. *Perfect.*

The woman was beautiful, no getting around that plain truth. So why had she answered an ad in a mail-order bride catalogue and traveled across the wilds of Texas to find a husband? If the Bible she was clutching was any indication, it could be that no man in the Fort Worth area wanted to be preached to any more than he did.

Dread lowered over him. "Fine," he grunted. "But let me make it clear once more before we set out: I specifically asked for no Bible thumpers," He paused, letting his words have time to soak in before adding, "But Sophie needs a mother, so I will make an exception. However, I insist that you keep your beliefs to yourself, Is that clear?"

She bit her full, delicate bottom lip as she studied him, her blue eyes darkening. His pulse picked up again looking at her lips. Meeting her gaze, he knew she'd caught him staring.

She smiled sweetly and a dimple appeared, creasing her left cheek. Her eyes twinkled mischievously, and Mathew nearly fell off the wagon seat.

"Are you always this grumpy and disagreeable, Mathew McConnell?" she asked in that lilting voice.

Feeling as cantankerous as old Prudence, the mule that claimed his ranch as her own, he grunted again, unable to form words to answer her.. He was still trying to get past that dimple and that smile. And those lips.

Befuddled, Mathew looked straight ahead. "Yah!" He cracked the reins, inclining the horses to travel at a faster pace. Melvina chuckled. Her laughter was a soft tinkling sound in the hot breeze.

She was determined, that was for sure. A good thing since determination was the one quality a woman especially needed in order to survive this frontier.

That and the ability to laugh even when things were tough. He glanced at Melvina. Her chin was lifted into the wind, her eyes bright as she took in her surroundings, and a smile lingered on her lips. He knew Melvina had that ability too, to laugh in hard times. He could sense it in her. So, she might do alright here in Texas after all.

Right then and there he resolved he'd offer this

woman his last name and his protection in exchange for care for his daughter. But not his love. Not his heart.

* * *

"Lands sakes, what a beauty!"

The plump older woman startled Ellie by bursting from the small whitewashed house. She limped slightly, skirts flapping, as she rushed to meet them.

"Maggie Sorenson," Matthew said, "This is Miss Melvina Eldora Smith."

"Well, I *certainly* hope so." The woman took Ellie's hand tenderly smiling as if she hadn't seen another woman in months. "I didn't figure you found another woman between here and the stagecoach stop, Matthew! It's so good to meet you Miss. Smith."

Mathew began tending to the horses, giving Ellie a moment to relax—she might have teased him about being cantankerous but it had been purely a way to hide the shaky way she'd felt when his gaze had paused on her lips. Pushing the thoughts away, Ellie focused on

Maggie, she liked the older woman instantly. "So good to meet you too. Mrs—"

"Maggie. Just plain Maggie," Maggie harrumphed, waving her hand. "I ain't one fer such uppity nonsense."

Maggie's refreshing welcome touched Ellie's heart, so unlike Aunt Millicent and the way she'd clung to formality like a shield. A renewed sense of freedom washed over Ellie and she smiled. "Then I'm Ellie. Just plain Ellie."

Mathew almost broke his neck jerking around to stare at her. "*Ellie*? I thought it was Melvina."

"I like it," Maggie interrupted. "It suits ya. Ain't that right, Mathew?"

"I should have spoken up sooner," Ellie said. "Aunt Millicent insisted I use Melvina. But I prefer Ellie." Matthew turned back to his horses, fumbling with the leathers and then moving to the far side of the team. Maggie seemed to enjoy seeing him flustered. Smiling, Ellie realized she enjoyed it too.

Mister Clute had been the one who'd shortened Eldora to Ellie, He said the plucky name fit her more.

And it did. He'd been the only one to call her Ellie, though she'd taken it up when thinking of herself. Now she was beginning a new life and she knew now she wanted to completely leave Melvina Eldora behind. As Ellie she could enjoy having the freedom to be herself. And that was a wonderful thought.

CHAPTER FOUR

Sitting on the floor beside the kitchen table, holding a rag doll and sucking her thumb was a rosy-faced little girl with big blue eyes and a curly blonde cap of hair that looked as soft as her puffy pink cheeks.

"Oh!" Ellie froze in the doorway. Joy bloomed inside of her at the sight of the beautiful child.

Tears filled her eyes. "Is this Sophie?"

Maggie beamed. "You two were made for each other. Why the child even looks like you."

Ellie scarcely heard Maggie, she was too intent on the child.

Sniffing, she blinked away the tears of joy and thanked God for leading her here. She could endure whatever was to come for the chance to be a mother to this motherless child.

Sophie popped her thumb from her mouth and gave a toothless smile. "Doll," she held up her doll to Ellie.

Ellie knelt, tucked her skirts beneath her and leaned close to Sophie. "She's a very pretty doll," she said, touching the rag dolls threaded hair then touching Sophie's curls too. "You are beautiful, Sophie."

Sophie touched Ellie's cheek tenderly. Maggie clucked her tongue and looked at Ellie. "She's two years old and doesn't try to talk much. I'm a little worried about that. Sophie, this is your mama," she said, grunting as she stooped down.

Ellie sucked in a sharp breath. She wasn't married to Mathew yet, so strictly speaking she wasn't her mama yet. However, from the moment she'd read his ad in the *Hitching Post* Ellie's heart had been lassoed tight to this child. There was no letting go.

"*Ma*-ma," Sophie said, smiling up at Ellie. She stood and reached out with her damp hand to grab a fistful of Ellie's blond curls. "Mama."

"Wonderful." Maggie beamed at Sophie's words.

Ellie reached for the baby and cuddled her close. When Sophie giggled Ellie knew this was as close to heaven as she would ever feel here on earth. Ellie's arms tightened on the child, and she felt the hope of love. All of Ellie's life she'd longed for love of another human being, longed to know what it would feel like. If she lavished love on Sophie there was hope that Sophie would return that love.

And if she did the same to Mathew there was a chance... Surely love could blossom. She just had to play by his rules, and be a *good* wife and there was hope. Always hope.

"Maggie, thanks for watching Sophie," Mathew's strong voice broke into Ellie's thoughts.

Putting one hand on her knee Maggie pushed up from her kneeling position. Her grimace of pain made it easy to tell the action was hard on her.

"You're welcome. I'm happy you've got this pretty little gal to soon call wife. Look at how your baby girl has taken to her new ma."

Hugging Sophie to her, Ellie smiled when the child's pudgy hand let go of her hair and flattened gently against her cheek. Her heart tightened at the touch and dug deep, the bond strong and swift. Mathew was unsmiling as he studied them. His dark eyes emotionless and his full wide lips flattened in a grim line. Unease quivered in her belly.

"I think our Mathew isn't good at smiling," she quipped nervously, her gaze darting from him to Maggie who had punched her fist to her ample hips and was studying Mathew as well. At Ellie's words Maggie threw back her head and hooted with laughter.

"Pegged him right off, ya did, Ellie. Our Mathew is scarce on smiles and even more scarce on talk." She grinned. "I think with that sparkle of mischief I see in your blue eyes you might just be the one to tug both from the depths of him."

Mathews brows dipped. Once again Ellie thought the man cute with that scowl on his handsome face. But there was trouble in his eyes.

What pain was he fighting behind all of those

scowls and gruff words?

"She's darling, Mathew. Just a sweet, sweet girl," she said.

He'd removed his hat upon entering and now he tapped it against his thigh. "Then, I guess we should be going over to the pastor's place."

"Mercy sakes this is a great day," Maggie said. "A great day indeed. Well, what are you waiting for Ellie? Jump up and get yourself hitched to that handsome lump of smiles standing over there."

Ellie stood and glanced again at Mathew, nope, she hadn't missed it.

He was not smiling.

The man, when not scowling, was probably the most handsome man Ellie had ever seen. Something about him, that chiseled jaw, those dark fathomless eyes that seemed to penetrate every dark corner of her being when he looked at her. That long lean body... Yes, Mathew McConnell by far took the most handsome man prize, and she was about to be his wife. It was amazing. But that being said, the man would obviously not have any trouble finding a wife. She hadn't missed the way the few ladies she'd seen walking along the streets of Wishing Springs looked at him. So why had he resorted to sending that letter to *The Hitching Post*? She knew why she had. But why him?

She was suddenly struck by how alone he looked standing in that doorway.

Maybe he was heartbroken. Maybe he would always love his first wife. Maybe that was why God had led her here. *Maybe* she was here to help him smile again. Just like he and his baby were helping her have a new, bright future.

Ellie halted her runaway thoughts and stilled the nerves that were making her ramble on in her head.

Maybe she should just calm down. "*I will never leave you or forsake you...thus said the Lord...*" Her nerves eased down as she repeated Joshua 1:5 once more. She'd been repeating that verse all across Texas, tossing and bumping inside that stagecoach bound for this. The good Lord had repeated Himself to Joshua *four times* to get it through to him. And Joshua being such a mighty man of God and all, she wasn't feeling too bad that she needed far more reminders than four.

"I'm ready—*we're* ready," she added, hugging Sophie tightly, then she followed Mathew out the door.

* * *

Less than an hour after leaving Maggie's with Melvina and Sophie, Mathew was standing in the preacher's small study staring down into her disconcerting blue eyes. There was trust in those eyes and it unsettled him more than he wanted it to. She'd said to call her Ellie, but he'd continued to call her the more formal Melvina. She'd been startled when he'd done this, but she'd yet to mention it. He was glad. The last thing he wanted to explain to her was that calling her Ellie would be far more personal than he felt comfortable with.

"Take hands please," Reverend Jacobs instructed.

Melvina lifted her hand, hesitated, and then, holding his gaze, she held it out to him. Swallowing a lump that suddenly lodged in his throat, Mathew took her slender fingers in his.

"Melvina Eldora Smith, do you take this man, Mathew McConnell, to be your lawfully wedded husband?" Reverend Jacobs asked, his deep voice reverberating through the small room.

Mathew felt Melvina's hand tense in his. Her fingers trembled slightly and her gaze faltered momentarily before she nodded, and a small gentle smile appeared. "I do," she said, at last.

Mathew's heart weighed heavy in his chest.

"Mathew McConnell, do you take this woman, Melvina Eldora Smith as your lawfully wedded wife, promising to love, honor and protect her in sickness and in health, till death do you part?" Mathew tried not to think about the word love as he nodded his head then spoke clearly. "I do."

In his heart of hearts he knew he could do everything the oath required except offer his love. Love had never been part of the deal. However, looking into Melvina's eyes and seeing the sweet smile she gave him, he felt an unreasonable tug of guilt.

This was a practical marriage he reminded himself. He'd stated it clearly from the beginning. Why then he wondered as the Reverend Jacobs pronounced them husband and wife, did he feel like he'd just done something terribly wrong?

* * *

"There's the house."

They'd just rounded a bend in the dusty track that wove through a stand of oaks. A hawk watched them from one of the tallest trees and a couple of red birds played tag against the blue sky. Ellie had been so lost in thought that she'd been missing the beauty surrounding them.

Tall, full oaks grew in clumps through expanses of scraggly mesquite trees. Ranch land stretched out from there, and they'd passed several streams where longhorn cattle grazed nearby and drank their fill. Mathew had told her these were his cattle and his ranch land. She'd been startled by the size of it. Dusk was setting in. He'd said when he had hurried her from Maggie's that they'd have to be quick with the ceremony in order to make it to the house before nightfall.

He hadn't been joking. His ranch was about three

miles from town but that was just to the boundary of it. If Ellie had wanted to live in the country she was getting her wish.

"It's lovely." Built from stone and plank, the tidy-looking one-story house had a wide, welcoming porch. The front door was flanked by windows on either side and weathered gray. Both end of the house had a large stone chimneys.

"Did you build this?" she asked, amazed.

"I hope it will do," Mathew said, not looking at her. "Because there's too much work on the ranch needing my attention right now to be able to take time to change anything."

"Change, why? It is absolutely the most charming place in the world. It's amazing." She and Aunt Millicent had lived in the home she'd been born in—the home her mother died in. Though it was nice it had had been far too stuffy for Ellie's taste. Over the years her aunt had been forced to take in sewing and had opened a dress store in the front parlor. She kept the rest of the house as a sort of shrine to the years she'd lost before Ellie had destroyed all their lives.

Ellie discovered the inside of the ranch house was just as impressive. It was easy to see that a woman had helped put the house in order with the cozy way the spacious living room and kitchen were situated. Three chairs and the wall bench were to one side anchored in a warm, inviting way by a colorful rag rug and pillows that blended with it. The kitchen table was long and hand built from the gnarled trunks of the abundant mesquite trees and the table top made of oak.

On the opposite side of the house from the kitchen with its big stone fireplace was another room. Mathew carried in her valise into that room. She followed him and stopped dead in her tracks, clutching the still sleeping Sophie in her arms. The room was dominated by a fireplace that was smaller than the kitchen's and a large bed that sat next to a single window. There were no colorful rugs on the floor or pillows in the rocking chair that sat in the corner by the baby bed. Even so, the room drew her in and shook her insides up like nothing she'd ever experienced as dawning suddenly began to set in...this was their bedroom.

Mathew set her valise down at the foot of the bed

then moved past her to the door. "I'll bring your chest in after I take care of the livestock." And then he was gone. And it was a good thing since Ellie felt certain he could hear her reckless heart making an outlandish racket inside her chest.

Where would Mathew sleep?

Oh goodness, she'd been so caught up in Sophie and the wedding that her nerves about...her wedding night had somehow shrunk to the recesses of her mind.

Crossing the room, she kissed Sophie on the forehead and gently placed her in her bed. Then, chewing her bottom lip, she eyed that big stuffed bed.

CHAPTER FIVE

Mathew was holding a pitchfork full of hay when Melvina stormed into the barn. Despite the sun having dipped low and the dim light in the barn her eyes flashed fire.

"I need to get something straight, something I somehow overlooked in my excitement of the day," she said, wringing her hands as she spoke, her cheeks flushed.

He tossed the hay over the stall to the milk cow, then jabbed the fork into the ground and leaned his elbow on the end of the handle. "Okay," he said, not sure at all what to make of this outburst.

"I…I need some time to...before..." She paused, her hand coming up to touch one of her burning cheeks.

Alarm hit him. "Are you feeling ill?"

"No. I need...Oh fiddle." She stomped her foot and stuffed her hands to her slim hips. "I'm not ready."

"Ready? For what?"

"I hadn't expected to share a room with you immediately," she blurted.

"Share a room?"

"Yes, I...I thought there would be two rooms. I...I've only known you for a few hours."

Her meaning dawned on him finally. "I moved my things into the tack room yesterday."

"Oh," she squeaked. "I see."

Her gaze swung to the door of the tack room. It was opened just enough that the cot could be seen. "It's not much of a room."

He hitched an eyebrow at her. "Until I have time to add on another room at the house, it will do."

Her head snapped. "Another room?"

"Another room, Melvina. I married you to be a mother to Sophie. That's all."

Her brows crinkled and her chest moved up and

down rapidly as she took several quick breaths. Her hands came to her cheeks, then dropped to her sides. "I see," she said, quietly. "Right. A *practical* wife." Then she turned and walked briskly back the way she'd come.

He knew he should go after her. Explain. Instead, he stood in the middle of the barn he'd built for the life he'd planned to have with Beth. He'd needed a mother for Sophie. He planned to keep her around. He'd married Melvina, given her his name and his protection. He wouldn't risk her life, or his heart—not this time. Not ever again.

No, he'd learned his lesson well. This was all he had to give.

* * *

Standing outside exploring her surroundings with Sophie on her hip, Ellie still couldn't believe it had been a week since she'd married Mathew and become Sophie's mother. Looking up at the summer sun, its heat pelting down on them she felt its warmth radiating through her. Though things weren't exactly as she'd expected them to be, it had been the best week of her life.

"There's my good girl," Ellie laughed swinging a giggling baby Sophie into her arms. Sophie was a dream and taking care of her filled Ellie's heart to bursting.

Then again, Sophie's daddy had her wanting to burst something over his head! She'd tried to help with taking care of the chores around the yard like milking the cow and feeding the chickens. Mathew had told her a stern no. He'd said that taking care of Sophie and the household chores like washing and cooking should keep her plenty busy. He'd take care of the rest. She'd almost told him she'd spent time on Mister Clute's ranch but she was trying so hard not to be argumentive, to be the wife Mathew wanted, that she'd held back and done as he'd asked.

Ellie had so looked forward to being a rancher's wife and getting involved with the ranching side of things. Even helping to round up cattle and such—but he'd cut her off before she could tell him that.

Not that she wasn't having a wonderful time with Sophie—she was. But…she'd hoped to fulfill her secret passion too.

Besides, without help, Mathew was hardly around and that wasn't good for Sophie either. Ellie wondered if he was avoiding them because of the way she'd confronted him about the household arrangements. The encounter had knocked her off solid ground and she was shaken. She hadn't wanted to just jump right into the rights of a husband on the very first day that they had met and married. However…she hadn't counted on never knowing Mathew as a husband. On never carrying a child of her own. The discovery stung like a slap.

And he was barely around, leaving early in the mornings and showing up late each night to grab a bite before disappearing to his quarters.

Yet she thought about him almost every minute of the day. It was maddening.

"We're doing fine, Sophie. Just you and me," Ellie said.

"Pru-dy!" Sophie squealed, just as the rumble of hooves sounded behind them.

Spinning around, Ellie was shocked to see a brown mule charging toward them. The hairy beast barreled down on them with the speed of a wild mustang, lips pressed back, huge teeth bared.

Ellie screamed, hugging Sophie to her chest. Ellie raced toward the closest building, the barn. She had to protect Sophie. She had too!

"Pru-dy!" Sophie squealed again, looking over Ellie's shoulder. *Is she trying to say pretty?* Ellie wondered as she ran. Or tried to run, her skirts tangled against her legs. Thick and cumbersome, the dratted clothing had her tripping and shuffling as she ran. Holding the armload of child to her, she didn't have extra hands to hold them up—petticoats were a curse!

Ellie had made it past the watering trough when she tripped and pitched forward. Trying to protect Sophie, Ellie twisted around and hit the ground on her back. The air whumphed out of her in a rush so strong she couldn't get it back. Gasping for new air, struggling, Ellie could only flounder helplessly on the ground, flat on her back unable to breathe.

Laughing, unaware of the danger befalling them

Sophie sat on top of Ellie and clapped her pudgy hands together. Ellie heaved for air as the child giggled and the crazed mule plowed toward them. Just when Ellie thought they would be trampled for certain, the animal slid to a halt, plopped down on its haunches and began to lick Sophie's cheek!

* * *

Mathew had lost more cattle. He'd found a spot where his fence had been deliberately cut. He was certain he had rustlers. He just had to find them. But right now he was headed home. He had to talk to Melvina.

He'd hurt her somehow. He could see the hurt in her eyes this morning.

And it ate at him all day.

But he didn't know how to fix it. He could only offer her what he had to give and that wasn't his heart. He'd topped the last hill for home when he spotted Prudence thundering toward Melvina with baby Sophie in her arms. Mathew spurred his horse to a gallop, hoping to intercept the alarmed mule. But he'd been too far away to prevent the scene before him and could only watch Ell—*Melvina* flying across the yard like someone had lit a fire to her skirt.

Mathew arrived just after she flipped to the ground like a flapjack. He threw himself from the saddle, despite the almost at a full gallop, hitting the ground at a run. "Ellie, are you alright?" he asked, sliding to a stop he pushed Prudy away. It was a hard thing to do since the mule thought Sophie was half hers.

Ellie's eyes were wide as she struggled for air to breathe, wheezing and gasping for air.

The fall must have knocked her breath out of her. He lifted Sophie from her chest in the hopes that lacking the weight of the plump baby girl would enable her to breathe again. "Come on Ellie, take a breath," he urged gently. With his guard down because of his concern, calling her Ellie slipped naturally into place. It was more personal than he'd wanted to allow them to get, but felt right. Partly because the name did fit her personality.

Seconds later Ellie sucked in a deep breath and sat up with his help. She glared at the mule sitting calmly beside her on its fat haunches. "What—is that animal doing?" she asked in a shrill voice he'd never heard before.

"Protecting Sophie," he said, sheepishly.

"Protecting her! She almost killed us."

Glaring at him, she clamped her lips together and stood up. He tried to help her but she ignored his hand, gave the unconcerned little mule one last glare, then stomped stiffly toward the house.

Should he follow her? She was one mad lady—and she had a right to be.

Carrying Sophie who was chanting, "Pru-dy, Pru-dy," all the way, he stalked after her. He caught up to her at the porch.

"I should have warned you about old Prudence. That cantankerous donkey thinks she owns the place. And she watches out for Sophie. She's been out with a herd protecting the baby calves from coyotes, but we moved the herd closer this morning and she must have wanted to see Sophie." Now that the danger was over his mind went straight back to Ellie running from the funny old gray bag of bones. He couldn't help himself—he chuckled.

Red as a ripe plum, Ellie gasped. "You are *laughing* at me!"

He tried not to laugh again. Fought hard not to, a hard thing to do when suddenly all he could think about was how cute the woman looked when she was furious. "Now, Ellie...calm down. You do have to admit that it was funny."

"I do not!" She crossed her arms.

He hiked a brow and grinned.

"Fun-ny," Sophie repeated and giggled.

His chest hurt with the laughter he was holding back. He was a little worried about her reaction at his finding this so blamed funny, but it just was. And she was cute as a baby porcupine when she was mad.

"Ellie. You know it was funny."

"Fun-ny, fun-ny," Sophie said proudly and clapped.

Ellie's lip twitched, causing his smile to widened.

"You know it's true. You would have laughed if it had been me in your shoes. You can't hold this against me too."

She bit her lips, both sides twitched and suddenly she laughed, dipped her head and hooted.

Hearing her full-bodied laugh pulled the first full blown laugh from him that he'd had in two years. It hit him as he smiled at her. It felt good watching her laugh so hard tears rolled from the corners of her sparkling eyes. She rubbed them away with her fingers then pressed them to her cheeks.

"You are mean, Mathew McConnell. And I think you have a really terrible sense of humor."

"And you've got Sophie laughing at me too."

"Me laughing too," Sophie quipped.

Ellie's smile as she scolded him reached inside of Mathew, warming the dark corners of his heart.

He stopped laughing and they stared at each other as if they couldn't look away.

Mathew's heart was doing crazy things in his chest. Like a crazy fool, he stepped closer to Ellie, tempted to reach his hand out and trace the line of her jaw. Instead, he clutched Sophie tightly.

"I have to go," he blurted, and pushed Sophie into Ellie's arms. Snagging the leathers of his horse as he passed he gave himself a good talking-to all the way to the barn and into the safety of the shadows inside. *What had I been doing?*

Wondering what it would feel like to pull her into his arms and pretend that this was a real marriage.

"You are downright loco," he growled, his heart thumping and his blood rushing through his ears like the rapids of the Guadalupe river.

CHAPTER SIX

"I'm a fool. I'm a fool—Yes I am. Yes I am," Ellie sang her frustrations in a sweet singsong voice as she held Sophie in the air and looked up at the grinning, drooling sweetheart. "How could I be such a fool, Sophie sweetie? How?"

"Foo-wel," Sophie repeated drooling more as she stared down happily at Ellie. "I mam a foo-wel."

Despite her own angst, Ellie laughed and hugged her baby to her heart. No, she wasn't a fool for having come three hundred miles through dangerous territory to marry a man who *just* needed someone to watch his child. Not when that child was this angel.

Walking to the big wooden rocker sitting by the window, Ellie tucked a chattering Sophie in the crook of her arm and began to sing a lullaby. At least Sophie was everything she'd dreamed of, she thought as Sophie's bright blue eyes began to droop with the motion of the rocker. Soon, her face went slack with sweet release into dream time. Ellie could watch Sophie sleep all day.

Sighing, Ellie brushed a blonde curl from her forehead and then stared out the window. The mule watched her from a few feet away. Ellie was not feeling very forgiving at the moment and did not look kindly on the hairy beast!

She had more interesting things on her mind. Mathew had begun calling her Ellie and he'd almost kissed her out there, before he stormed away. She was certain of it. Ellie's heart fluttered as she relived the moment when he'd leaned forward…

For a girl who'd never been close to having someone look at her that way, it was almost more than she could bear. More than she could hope.

And then he'd spun and strode away as if he couldn't get away fast enough.

"Please Lord help me. I am so confused," she whispered. Bowing her head Ellie did what she'd learned to do growing up. She prayed. She thanked Him for his blessings, for Sophie and for Mathew and being here at all. She told God her fears about her situation and her desires and at last she asked God to give her patience that she would let Him show her the way.

Lifting her gaze, she stared out the window once more.

Patience was not easy for her, in this situation especially. She wanted things to move faster than they were. But she had no idea how to do that. She'd tried everything she could think of—making small talk, not talking at all, trying to simply show him what a wonderful wife she could be if he let her. Her nerves were shot.

She wanted that kiss from her husband.

She'd wanted it with all of her heart.

There she had admitted it. Admitted that she longed

to feel his arms around her and his lips on hers.

Aunt Millicent would be appalled.

But he was her husband. And Aunt Millicent's opinion of her no longer mattered she reminded herself. Mathew strode from the barn, drawing Ellie's attention.

Carrying a saddle, he looked as though he could fight the world itself.

He tramped across the yard toward the corral that sat a little ways away from the house. Several horses were kept there and he'd told her early on that they were horses he was going to break and for her to keep Sophie away from them.

He dropped the saddle in the dirt. Entered the pen and within seconds had a particularly irritated black horse roped. Looking wildly angry, the colt snorted and pawed the earth. Mathew gave it some slack as it yanked its head violently. Ellie's breath caught when it reared up, standing on two legs, its front hooves clawing dangerously at Mathew!

* * *

"Today is your day," Mathew said to the two-year-old colt with a very bad attitude. Mathew was brewing to release some frustration. From the looks of it, Ruthless was too.

He'd worked with the colt for a few days and he was still skittish and untrusting. Straining against the rope, Ruthless pawed the earth and reared up as Mathew held on to to the rope, his arms straining as dirt flew as they fought each other. Mathew wound the rope around the breaking pole and snugged the angry horse so close to it that he couldn't so much as lift his head. Still the stubborn horse kicked up dirt and dug at the ground with his hooves. Breathing hard from the fight, Mathew got the bit and bridle on him—no easy task. Then he headed out of the corral for the saddle. He was already damp from exertion, and the frustration he felt from his situation with Ellie hadn't diminished at all...

Mathew welcomed the challenge.

Ruthless offered an avenue for him to vent—

"What are you *doing*?"

Mathew whirled around to find Ellie, looking wild-eyed herself.

"What are you doing out here?" he snapped. He needed to get rid of his frustration, not pile on more.

She pointed at the colt. "Are you about to ride him?"

"That's the plan," he said, not happy to see her *or* her attitude. "If Ruthless is willing"

"Willing to kill someone," Ellie scoffed.

Her lack of confidence stung. "No one's dying today, Ellie."

"That is not funny. It looks like he needs more time. More work before you haul off and climb on his back."

"Ellie, what do you know about ranching? Nothing, that's what. You tend to woman's work and leave man's work to me."

"But—"

"No, Ellie, get on back to the house and leave me be," he snapped. At this point he was so frustrated he was past caring.

Her eyes shadowed. Beautiful eyes that had him

losing his train of thought all over again even in his anger.

"That isn't fair. Mathew, I can help. I haven't been given the chance to show you what I can do."

This land was not easy on a woman. His mother and then with Beth were proof, and also Maggie and the way she was breaking down with her joints and ailments. "No" the word wrenched from him. "I hired you—I mean I married you to look after Sophie."

Ellie went very still and the color drained from her face.

Mathew knew he'd made a big mistake the moment he'd said "hired." If he'd been too dumb to realize his blunder, the grim look spreading across Ellie's face would have pointed it out to him straightaway.

"Hired me! Hired me. Of all the…" She faltered on the last, huffing so hard he was sure he saw smoke come out of her ears. She spun and stalked back the way she'd come.

They sure did do some stalking away from each other, he thought as her skirts flounced and her hips swayed. She muttered halfway across the yard. He couldn't understand what she was saying, but it was obvious that it wasn't good. She was pert near to the porch when she swung back around and stalked straight back to him.

She didn't stop until she was toe to toe with him, so close she had to tilt her head back to glare up at him.

"You might look at me as just a hired hand, but Mathew McConnell, I have news for you—you married me! That's right. We are lawfully wedded in the sight of man and God, and I'm tired of tiptoeing around here not knowing where I fit in. I've done that all my life. I came west to get rid of that feeling. I am your wife. An—and I'm here to tell you that I want children. I want brothers and sisters for Sophie. You may not want me like a husband should want a wife—or want this marriage to be real. But..." Her voice trailed off. She looked at the ground and then back up at him. "I do. A real home and family is all I've ever dreamed of. Fair warning to you," she said, her hand on her hip. "I did not come here to be your hired help. Nor to be told what I can and cannot do"

And then she spun away and stormed back the way

she'd come.

Mathew watched her go. The woman was beauty and fire and sass all in one. He'd had to fight the urge to pull her into his arms and kiss her to silence. Instead, grabbing the saddle at his feet, he headed into the corral.

It was time to ride—he just hoped Ruthless was still ready for a fight, because he sure was.

CHAPTER SEVEN

Ellie stalked to the house. "*Hired* me?" Evidently taking a mail-order bride was Matthew's way of ensuring he kept the hired help on, forever. Wasn't this just the way? Here she'd just told the Lord she'd wait on his lead. That she'd be patient and just look at this fine mess.

Well, she'd gone and done it now. She'd hauled off and blasted Mathew with both barrels.

But she couldn't take back her words. They were true. In her heart of hearts she desired more children. Loving on Sophie had only made her want them more. *Mathew*—the man could irritate her so. And hurt her too.

Why was it that his words could hurt her like no one else's could?

Ellie stepped onto the porch and through the door. Heading toward her room where Sophie slept. Mathew McConnell thought he knew her—had judged from day one by the dress she'd worn and the Bible she'd held close to her heart. "Ha," she muttered, softly, entering the bedroom. Sophie was sound asleep. "Your daddy doesn't know me at all," Ellie whispered then headed to her trunk at the foot of the bed.

She was tired of hiding behind the stifling airs and proprietary manners that Aunt Millicent had always insisted on, being told all her life what she could and could not do!

It was time to be true to herself.

Lifting the lid of her traveling trunk, Ellie dug to the bottom through all the fluffy dresses Aunt Millicent loved. They went flying all directions as Ellie reached the bottom of the trunk.

Back home, Ellie had found herself following the creek to old Mister Clute's small ranch, which hadn't been too far from town, when she couldn't take Aunt

Millicent's never-ending rants any longer. It was there she'd discovered that she'd loved the country. There she'd begun to dream of life on a ranch.

Knowing she was going to be a part of a ranch had been an added bonus to accepting Mathew's proposal and fulfilling her dream.

All her life she'd been put down, told what to do…and rejected. The one person who'd accepted her had been old Mister Clute. She'd thought things would be different here, more like they'd been with her old neighbor. Mathew was treating her just as her Aunt had.

Ellie lifted her clothes from the trunk, the feel of them giving her fortitude.

It was a new day for Melvina Eldora Smith *McConnell*.

Mathew, the stubborn man, might think he was going to deny her all the dreams bulging inside her heart—but he had another think coming!

* * *

"Whoa there," Mathew snapped. Having gotten the

saddle on Ruthless' back without getting killed, the next step was getting on his back still alive. And that was the tricky part.

Easing his boot into the stirrup, he saw the colt's ears twitch, a sure sign the fight would be on. Ready to rid himself of clashing emotions raging in him, Mathew shoved his boot into the stirrup, threw his leg over and held on! The battle was on.

The horse was greener than green, as rank a ride as any Mathew had ever ridden. Ruthless, infuriated and fearful, reacted violently. Mathew knew deep in his heart that there was some fear in him too, that he and the horse had that in common. They were both fighting it one as much as each other.

The angry animal bucked and twisted and tried its best to unseat him. Lying back in the saddle, Mathew held on. Sweat poured from Mathew's brow. His muscles burned from using them all—his thighs, forearms, his gut –to stay in the saddle. Ruthless was not tiring, instead he kicked repeatedly, traveling about the corral like a Texas twister. Mathew had the skill to hang on and not eat dirt where the horse was concerned.

But, with Ellie he was buried neck deep in dirt.

Ruthless had him riding a wicked buck midair when movement out of the corner of Mathew's eye snagged his attention. A small person in baggie pants and a big shirt came flouncing out of his house, hat in hand, blond hair shining in the sunlight.

Her expression grim as she stalked his way.

Mathew was so startled he almost lost his seat. His hands went slack for a moment.

Ruthless took advantage of his distraction—immediately twisting into the fence scrapping Mathew's legs against the corral rungs. An instant of lost concentration was all it took for the horse to send Mathew flying from the saddle and straight over the top of the fence. Something struck him hard. Stars burst inside his head, bright and hot, and then he bit the dust.

The alarmed blue eyes of his wife staring down at him through a white rain of cascading stars was the last thing he saw before the world went dark.

I killed him!

"Mathew," Ellie cried, dropping to the dirt as she stared at his pale face. Blood spit at her from the gash on his head—it was a gusher!

Jerking her shirt tail out of her britches, she grabbed it between her teeth and yanked—and almost broke her teeth! The shirt was no thin petticoat and refused to rip.

Wishing for the first time in her life that she was wearing the ridiculous piece of clothing, Ellie panicked—she was just about to yank off the shirt and hold it to his forehead when she spied his knife in its holder tied to his belt. Fumbling for it with trembling hands, Ellie freed it from its home and stabbed the blade into her shirt tail, slicing off a large section of fabric.

She wadded it up and held it firmly over the wound.

She'd seen head wounds before, and prayed it would stop after a few minutes. This was her fault. She'd gone and let her temper, her pent-up rebellion, get the best of her.

She'd thrown her prayers and promises of patience out the window and let herself take control.

Poor Mathew. He'd been so startled at seeing her dressed in her britches that he lost concentration. He was beautiful in the saddle, a born rider, and she'd done him in with a pair of britches.

Not even considering that her timing for a confrontation could wait until he was off the dangerous animal, oh no, she'd stormed outside determined to have her way right then and there..

And just look what it had gotten her...very likely a soon-to-be dead husband!

"I've mourned the day you were born, Melvina. Good riddance and woe to the man who takes you in." Her aunts last parting words as she'd climbed aboard the stage echoed in the recesses of her heart. So thrilled to be on her way, and so hardened to the bitter words of her aunt, Ellie never considered that she might well and truly bring catastrophe to her new family. Tears and fear clogged in her throat. *Murderin Melvina.*

"Please don't die," she whispered, watching the blue cloth turn a dark read. "Dear Lord, please, *please* stop this bleeding." Her prayer rang out loud and pleading as her fingers turned sticky with Mathew's blood. "I'm no good to anyone. I've been here a week and already added my husband to my list of...of...dead." She eked the last word weakly.

Looking at the pale, oh so handsome face of her

near dead husband she knew the truth. She *was* born a killer.

Tears slipped from her eyes. Lifting the soaked rag, she peeked at the gash. There was a knot forming there and the blood flow had eased. She willed him to open his eyes. Sweat made trails in the drying blood. She needed to cool him down.

Running to the water trough she filled a bucket and hurried back. No time to boil the water. Taking his knife she sliced off the other side of her big shirttail. She dipped it into the cool water and gently pressed the cloth to his forehead, careful to wipe around the wound and not over it. He moaned but didn't move. His dark lashes didn't even flicker.

She had to get him out of the scorching sun. Standing, she grabbed him under the arms. Grunting, she put her full weight into the effort. The man was six feet something and weighed far more than she did. He didn't budge. She planted her feet, took hold of him, and tried harder—throwing her whole body into pulling him. Straining, her hands slipped and she fell backward flat on her bottom in the dust.

Huffing, she wiped sweat from her brow and searched for help. Spotting Prudy watching her from the corner of the barn, Ellie's heart sparked with hope.

"Ah! Come here, pretty Prudy," she called, striding toward the mule. Prudence looked up, but didn't look too trustful. Ellie grabbed a rope hanging on a post by the barn and quickly making a loop, she threaded the rope through. Yes, thanks to Mister Clute, she wasn't as helpless as Mathew had thought her to be.

Whipping the rope to twirling above her head, she walked to the edge of the barn and let the rope fly. At the same instant, Prudy broke for clear pastures. Ellie had anticipated this and the rope landed perfectly around her neck—a fact Prudy did not like. Not in the least!

A horrible noise erupted from the animal as she continued running full blast for high country. But Ellie held tight to the rope. When the rope went tight, she was jerked off her feet, flying through the air briefly before landing in the dirt for the second time that day. Ellie held tight, though, Mathew's life depended on her. She was dragged behind the wildly circling mule, bouncing and bumping like a rag doll, dragged through dirt and rocks.,

When she hit a large bump, Ellie screamed, flopped over and stared at the sky as it raced by. Ellie's hand slipped, the rope jerked from her hand and only then did she realize her hand was wrapped in the rope. She was in a pickle now.

"Prudance, whoa, mule!" Mathew's deep commanding voice rang out.

He was alive. Ellie had never heard such a wonderful sound as his voice. Wanting to cry with joy, she cranked her head and saw him staggering to stand as she flew past him in a cloud of dirt.

"Hellllp me," she chattered, skidding over several rough patches. "Ow! Oh!" She'd be mortified if she wasn't in so much pain!

"Prudence, halt this minute, you stubborn mule," Mathew bellowed.

To Ellie's relief Prudy arched her path toward the barely standing cowboy, slowed and trotted his way.

CHAPTER EIGHT

Ellie would have flung her arms around Mathew's neck if she could move.

And the sky would stop spinning.

"Are you alright?" he asked, blood covered and glorious to Ellie. "What in the world are you doing?" He looked a little unstable as he reached down, grimacing and tugging the rope from around her aching hand. When she was free, he held his hand out to her. "Can you stand?"

She reached for his offered hand. "Thank you," she managed, as they both staggered while she gained her feet. "You were out cold and bleeding like a waterfall," she said, staring into his dazed eyes. "I was trying to get

Prudy to help me get you out of the sunlight."

"You were doing a fine job of it too." A grin tipped his lips as he swayed. She feared he wasn't going to make it upright long.

"Funny," Ellie said, woozy herself she wrapped an arm around his waist. Pulling his arm across her shoulders, she forgot the pain of her bumps and bruises the instant she realized she was snuggled up against him.

"Walk, cowboy. We need to get you in the house before you pass out again."

"Why, thank you little lady," he said, sounding odd, his speech slurred and his feet fumbling beneath him.

If she hadn't known better she'd say the man was drunk. He was trying to help, trying to support some of his weight as they swayed and weaved their way to the house with Prudy trailing them.

Something wasn't right.

They managed to make it up the step onto the porch and then through the doorway. From the back room she could hear Sophie crying. The wails so distraught that Ellie knew she'd been crying for a while.

From the yard, Prudy joined in the melee, hee-hawing her unhappiness of being left outside.

Ellie concentrated on getting Mathew to the bedroom, praying he wouldn't collapse before they made it to the bed.

Poor Sophie was standing up in her crib when they entered, her face stained with tears. Thankfully she calmed down when she saw them. "Mama," she hiccupped, as she watched them stagger past her toward the big bed. Ellie's heart melted even as she struggled to get the baby's pa settled.

"Here we go, ease on down here," Ellie commanded gently, her hand splayed out across his flat stomach as she eased him to sit on the side of the bed. He swayed as he sat. Their faces were so close she could feel his breath on her skin. His eyes dazed and a little crazy looking held hers. Grinning lazily, he touched her cheek.

"You sure do look pretty," he murmured, and before she knew what was happening he pressed his lips to hers.

Ellie's breath caught at the tenderness of his touch. Wonder and bliss, her first kiss! The longing for love filled her as she joined in, timidly at first and then with gusto. Suddenly Mathew's lips stilled and to Ellie's disbelief he pitched backward—passing straight out he hit the mattress like a rock!

His eyes closed, his breathing even...and a broad smile upon his face.

* * *

Someone was banging cast-iron skillets inside his skull.

Easing his eyes open, Mathew squinted at the ceiling and tried to get his bearings. He remembered Ellie coming out of the house in man's clothes and Ruthless taking him to task at the corral fence.

Things were fuzzy after that. Just like his head. He lifted a hand off the bed—bed? He was on his bed. How had that happened?

He moved to sit up when a wave of dizziness slammed into him.

Ellie padded into the room, the sound a loud echo in his skull. "You're awake. I was so worried. How do you feel?"

He tried to focus. There were *two* Ellies. Which he thought was nice since she was so pretty; it didn't hurt to have two of her to look at.

"If the room would stop spinning I'd be happier." He closed one eye—nope still two. Both Ellies planted their hands on their hips. He could see a faint flush on her cheeks. Both sets, Ellie One and Ellie Two. His head ached and he reached to rub his temple—

"No!" they cried, rushing forward. Ellie one grabbed his hand and tugged it away from his head.

"I feel weird," he mumble. Looking down, he saw blood on his shirt.

"You hit your head, Matthew. You can't rub it or the bleeding will start again."

Bleeding. He had a flash of Ellie's arms wrapped around him.

"What happened?" He fought a wave of nausea.

"You were thrown from that horse and hit your

head on the rail over the gate. You bled something fierce and then you were baking in the sun…" The words rushed from Ellie and suddenly it all came back to Mathew in a wave.

Ellie in britches! Then coming to, he'd struggled to focus, seeing her throw a lasso on Prudy like she was a seasoned cowpoke!

"You can rope," he said. "And you got dragged by Prudy."

He looked her up and down. She still wore the britches and there was splattered blood all over her.

"Yes, well, I can explain that. First, though, I'm sorry. I didn't mean to startle you so with the change of clothes. I know your getting hurt was my fault. You saw me and almost got killed."

"Yup, it threw me." He gave a shrug and saw worry in all four of her beautiful eyes. He concentrated and finally the two Ellies merged into one. The pain began to recede just a bit. "Don't blame yourself. Ruthless is a tough colt with a mind of his own. I should have never let him sense I wasn't paying attention."

"No, it was my fault." She looked away. "You ride well... You really do."

Her eyes darted to meet his, instantly dropped to his lips, and Mathew's insides filled with longing and an overwhelming need to kiss her.

Kiss her. Their gazes locked and she turned pinker than a cherry blossom. The color crept from beneath the cotton shirt and spread up her slender neck and then her jaw and then those trembling lips—and suddenly Mathew was hit with a full-blown flashback of kissing Ellie!

"Ellie." He sprang to his feet, wobbled and slammed back down onto the bed. "I *kissed* you." No wonder she looked so embarrassed. He'd sat right here on this bed and kissed her. She'd been helping him and he'd kissed her.

And then he'd passed out.

He was such a knucklehead.

Ellie stiffened, her jaw lifted. Her eyes flashed above flaming cheeks. "I *am* your *wife.*" Her eyes overly bright, she stomped loudly from the room.

Mathew wobbled. He'd really made a mess of things now and that was pure fact.

* * *

Ellie fought tears—she would not cry. Yes, she'd almost killed him, and she was truly indeed sorry for that. But he'd kissed her and passed out smiling, and left her with the most amazing feelings of hope and longing.

And then he hadn't even remembered it.

Reaching the stove, Ellie grabbed her rags and lifted the lid on the heavy pot of stew. Stewing herself, with the need to throttle her husband.

How dare the man look so insulted by the fact that he'd kissed her!

Married couples kissed. He didn't want to have a baby with her and he didn't want to kiss her. Ellie fought hard to not let this stab to her heart penetrate. But her heart had been weakened by his kiss—his wonderful, amazing kiss.

Tears slipped over the edge of her eyes. Drat them—she swatted at them with the cuff of her shirt.

She focused on Sophie playing and singing in the corner with her doll and a tin cup. She was here for Sophie, she was here for Sophie.

She sniffed. She would not cry.

"Ellie."

The air left her lungs—*Oh, dear Lord how long had he been standing there?*

"Ellie, look at me. Please."

She swiped at her eyes, hoping it would look as if she was pushing stray hair from her temples. Turning, she found Mathew just two steps away from her.

Gripping the back of the cane chair he was as pale as moonlight.

"You shouldn't be up," she admonished. "I, I was just about to bring you some stew." Ignoring the awkwardness coursing through her she slipped her arm around his waist. Instantly a wave of longing flooded her.

"You need to sit," she said, gruffly, her eyes downturned.

"No. I don't want to sit. Ellie, we need to talk."

"True," she agreed breathlessly. "We do. However, you falling out on the floor because you're too stubborn to sit down isn't going to help us get much talking done," she fussed. When she looked at him at last, his lips lifted into a darling crooked smile.

"Are you always so bossy?"

"Maybe," she hedged, looking away, her stomach dipping at his nearness...She was a lost cause. Her lips still burned from his kiss hours ago, and of their own accord her eyes sought his lips once more. He smiled. Her gaze flew upward to find him watching her.

Her heart kicked about so that it put Ruthless' ruckus to shame.

"Ellie. I haven't meant to hurt your feelings," he said gently, his fingers pushing a wayward strand of hair from her temple. "You have to understand there are some things I can't give a wife. I've tried to explain that but have done a poor job of it. One of those things is my heart, and because I can't give you all you deserve I won't take advantage of you."

Reality wrapped around her like a cold dark night.

She was unlovable; it was true after all.

"Please sit down, before you fall down," she urged, trying to resolve herself to what she'd never before been able to accept.

And she *really* couldn't handle it if he fell and the bleeding started up again.

He swayed and grabbed hold of Ellie, pulling her close. Ellie flung her arms around his waist and staggered, barely keeping him from toppling. Breathing hard, he held onto her, and when Ellie looked up his eyes were as wide as a full moon. Ellie felt faint—it was like an ailment or something when he was around!

Her head swam. He smelled of leather and pine, and Ellie realized she could breathe his scent for the rest of her life. The feel of his corded arms holding on to her was magical. Though he might not want her, he knew how to hold her so that she felt safe and wanted... Confusion tangled in her heart.

His arms tightened around her. She felt his heartbeat quicken against her own heart, and she thought he was going to kiss her again.

How could it be that he didn't want her and yet his kiss had been pure bliss?

Ellie's head spun with the delight of it. She closed her eyes and waited...Another moment ticked by, then he took hold of her arms and firmly set her away from him.

"We have to talk, Ellie."

CHAPTER NINE

Mathew yanked the other chair out from the table and sank into the one she'd pulled out for him earlier. "We have to talk—no getting mad and walking out. There are some things I've got to know."

Numb, Ellie sank into the seat. She felt as if she were the one who had struck her head. She was thankful for the gingham table cover she'd placed over the table that kept her shaking hands from his view.

"You're a beautiful woman, Ellie. I need to know what happened in your life to bring you here as a mail-order bride. And *where* did you learn to rope like that?"

With all they had to talk about—the kiss, the fact

that he didn't want her. And he wanted to talk about roping?

Unbelievably, relief washed over her, glad to have the moment to back away from the problems at hand. To find solid ground.

They were actually going to sit at the table and talk to each other. This was good.

The *Hitching Post* had set them up so quickly and there had only been a couple of letters between them. Both of their situations hadn't given them a lot of time to spend on a long correspondence. As things had turned out, she was certain Mathew hadn't seen her actual letters anyway. They'd been filled with her love of the Lord, and if he'd read them, he would have known she was a believer before she'd stepped off that stage.

"Well, it's a little embarrassing actually," she admitted.

"If we are going to become friends, and make this work then we should get comfortable with things. Even the embarrassing things."

Friends. Ellie couldn't speak for a moment as the very thought sank in…she'd so longed for a friend. She had told God she would be patient and then immediately she'd plowed forward and caused all this trouble. He was steadfast even in her fickleness.

Sophie crossed the room and grabbed her arm, smiling up at Ellie. Picking her up, Ellie breathed in the baby scent and cherished the way Sophie snuggled contently into the crook of her arm. Ellie met Mathew's eyes with courage.

"All my life I've been a little of a black sheep. You see, my mother died giving birth to me, so I have that in common with Sophie. Also, before the year was out my father died...Aunt Millicent said it was of a broken heart. He just couldn't take the loss of his beloved wife. My aunt said, he couldn't stand to look at me, so he left raising me up to her. A job she didn't want since she too grieved the loss of my mother, her younger sister. And then, her husband Mutt died not long after that. Uncle Mutt had started drinking because of the stress of having me to raise. And so when he was coming out of the saloon one night, he staggered in front of a runaway buggy and was killed." She'd gotten the story out without much emotion. "My aunt never let a day go by without reminding me of the misfortune I'd caused. And her friends' children picked up on what their parents were whispering about and teased me relentlessly."

Ellie had been looking down as she finished that part of her story.

"You were a child, Ellie," Mathew said softly. "None of that was your fault."

The fact that Mathew would even reassure her sent a gladness coursing through her.

"I know I'm not supposed to speak of it, but I can't talk about my past without telling what the Lord has done for me, Mathew. I found solace in His word. I've had to live with the consequences of those deaths, but the guilt for it doesn't belong to me." To her happiness, Mathew simply nodded when she'd said she needed to speak about her faith.

"You weren't responsible," he said, looking from her to Sophie.

"I've longed all my life to feel the closeness to a family that I've never known. When I came here I became pushy and a headstrong because I wanted it all so much. I was aggressive when I should have been patient. I'm sorry. I love—your child so much. And I'm so grateful to be here."

Mathew looked thoughtful.

Finally, with pain in his eyes, he said, "I'll admit that it's been hard for me to give my whole heart to Sophie. She reminds me so much of Beth. And it hurts looking at her sometimes and knowing what I lost. It shames me now, thinking about it. But I would never have treated her as you've been treated."

His words were quiet as he studied his child. Ellie's throat constricted with emotion as he touched Sophie's soft hair. "I needed someone to love her like I couldn't. That is why I let Maggie talk me into finding a mamma for her."

"Thank you for being honest," Ellie said. Sophie had taken hold of his finger and was chattering away to it as if she had lots to tell her pa's finger. It dug into Ellie's heart and caused an ache so strong Ellie knew she was here to help mend this relationship. *Thank you, Lord.* The prayer filled her and she smiled.

"You do love Sophie, Mathew. You just have to make peace with the past and open your heart to her."

He didn't say anything, though his eyes held a light she hadn't seen before.

"Tell me more of your life," he said, his eyes searching hers, digging deep. "And don't forget to tell me about this roping you've been hiding behind those frilly clothes."

No one had ever asked to talk to her of her life. Feeling suddenly light hearted she chuckled. "You are really worried about my britches. You see, my aunt was forced to find work after my uncle died. She opened a seamstress shop in the front parlor of our home and I was trained to help her at an early age. I started working in the shop almost before I could walk, picking up scraps of material and tidying up. And later I was trained to sew. Aunt Millicent and the ladies were overly fond of frills and ruffles and an overabundance of petticoats. I hated every minute of it I'm sorry to say. Cooped up in that house forever being reminded that I was the reason Aunt had to work to live. Every spare minute I could find I would escape to this small ranch not too far from town. Old Mister Clute owned it and he was getting up in age. He caught me trying to learn to ride one of his horses one day and took a shine to me. He wasn't much for words, but he taught me to rope and to ride. I'd even help him with his roundups because he was getting too old to get around."

"Well, I'll be," Mathew said, sitting back in shock.

"It's true. See, he'd lost his son in the war and closed off the world. These here are his son's clothes. He'd saved them in a trunk and he gave them to me. Those bothersome skirts were getting in my way and he knew it. They were getting dirty too and Aunt Millicent was getting furious about me going off and coming back filthy. It just made sense and helped keep our secret from her. She would have put a stop to my shenanigans if she'd known exactly what I was doing. Which she did when the truth came out three months ago."

Mathew leaned forward, looking much more stable than he had. "What happened when she found out? And how?"

"Mister Clute died." Sadness hit her. He'd been as close to a friend as she'd ever had. "His brother came and took over the ranch. When I asked him if I could help him out, he laughed at me and went straightaway and told Aunt Millicent. As you can imagine she was horrified that I'd been going behind her back, and especially that I would wear pants. She informed me that it was time for me to find my own way in life and stop embarrassing her. That said, she laid the *Hitching Post* on the table in front of me and told me to find a husband, preferably one that didn't live in Fort Worth."

"So it was your aunt's wish," Mathew said, clearly taken aback. "You didn't want this?"

Ellie shook her head. "Well, I was in shock at first. After a few minutes, I opened up the catalogue and immediately saw your ad. My heart latched onto your words as if you had written them directly to me. When I read how Sophie had lost her mama at birth, I felt drawn to her. I felt compelled by God to come so she would grow up feeling loved and wanted."

"Something you never felt," he said, gently.

The compassion in his voice caused her throat to knot up with emotion. She could only nod.

"I'm sorry you went through all of that." Mathew covered her hand with his, then stared at their hands while tracing his thumb slowly over her wrist. He swallowed hard, as if he too had a knot in his throat. After a moment he lifted sincere eyes to hers "Thank you for opening my eyes to the injustice I was doing to my daughter. Beth wouldn't have wanted me to give her baby any less than the love she would have lavished on her had she been alive." He smiled. "She would have liked you."

Joy flooded Ellie's heart. "I'm so glad. I hope you will want to tell Sophie of her mother when she is old enough. It will do her a world of good to know that her mother loved her."

They stared at each other for the longest moment, and though there was so much between them that was confusing and unfinished, this was ground to build on. Sophie deserved it.

"Mathew," she said, drawn to go on. "I need to tell you that I'm glad to be here. But I'm giving you fair warning that I just know God has a plan for my life. The Bible says He will give me the delights of my heart. And I've been holding on to that promise ever since I read your ad. It sustained me all the way here during that long stagecoach ride. And I'm not giving up on it now."

Mathew patted her hand like a brother and drew it away. Feeling him withdrawing emotionally, she stood, hoping she hadn't gone too far again. She wanted everything. Love, children, forever…and she knew he could see it in her eyes.

"How about some stew?" she said, breaking the connection. "It will help you feel better." She placed his daughter in his arms to anchor him to the chair since he seemed steady enough to stay upright now. "Love on your daughter for a few minutes while I get the meal ready. It will do you both a world of good."

CHAPTER TEN

"I ain't never seen nothin' like it," Lem said, a week after Mathew's accident.

"What's that Lem?" Mathew asked. They were searching for a couple of missing calves that Mathew hoped had just wandered off from their mothers. He was now certain he had rustlers systematically picking off his herd and he was going to have to put his attention to catching them soon.

"Maggie's got the notion to have a party. Says Ellie needs to be introduced around. And that's all fine and dandy to me, but you ain't never seen the likes of work that woman's got me doin'. Do this, Lem, do that. No, you ain't done it right—do it this way. I'm right fond of you and your new wife, but if this keeps up I ain't gonna be fond of my own much longer."

Mathew chuckled despite his wandering thoughts. Which kept going to Ellie as they had all week. His heart had cracked a little while Ellie told him about her past that night sitting at the kitchen table. How could her aunt be so cruel? So heartless? And how had Ellie survived it?

"Maggie comin' over the other day was a good thing. Ellie really enjoyed it."

Lem grinned. "Maggie, tried to put some of my britches on soon as we got home." He laughed. "You shoulda seen her. She looked like she'd been squeezed into a sausage skin."

Mathew chuckled, pretty sure Lem would be in a heap of trouble if Maggie knew he'd just told that on her. "You better watch out," he warned.

Lem hiked a bushy brow. "I told her I'd buy her a bigger pair if she wanted them, long as she'd start mucking out the stalls."

That got a hoot out of Mathew. "You said that and you're still walking around?"

"I can run faster than her with them bad knees of hers. And that there is the only reason—" He spat a stream of tobacco. "I'll tell ya that for sure. I hear Ellie's done taken over up at the house."

"She's taken over the chickens and milking the cow. And feeding the calves too. Her and Prudence have become fast friends. I'm telling you there was no holding her back once she'd yanked on those britches."

"Maggie said she was riding some too."

"Yup. She's riding some of the gentler stock I've broke, helping soften them up some more so they don't wild on me again. I worry, but she's a good rider, I have to admit. Tell you the truth she was born to be a rancher's wife. If it wasn't for Sophie, she'd be out here helping us right now."

"You told her 'bout the rustlers, though, right?"

"That's the only thing keeping her and Sophie from being out here. For Sophie's sake she's staying close to the house. She wants me to teach her to shoot a gun."

"Look out ever'body," Lem said, grinning widely.

"Yeah, that's what I said."

Lem sobered and he shook his head. "Mathew, I've

never heard of such as that Aunt of Ellie's."

So Ellie had confided her past to Maggie when she'd come for a visit. Mathew realized. Ellie suspected Ellie needed a woman to talk to and Maggie was the best.

"There are small minded people in this world," he said, shaking his head. "Ellie tries to make something good out of the injustice that was done to her." Her attitude made him ashamed of the hard time he'd given her when she got off the stage holding her Bible.

He wiped the sweat from his brow. They were heading down a ravine, their horses carefully picking their steps. "I've got to confess Lem. This is eating at me…I've known the love of my parents, and of Beth. Ellie hasn't known the love of anyone. She was barely tolerated by her aunt and then kicked out first chance the old bat got."

Lem looked over his shoulder, having moved in front on the narrow trail. "The two of you aren't—"

"I can't, Lem. It's just not in me." He had to admit sleeping on the lumpy mattress in the barn was getting old, especially when he thought about Ellie with her hair hanging loose and the feel of her soft lips against his—he stopped his thoughts in their tracks. No sense going down that road. Ellie had made it extremely clear she'd like more from their marriage—that she wanted children. But when he'd married her he'd vowed to protect her, and he aimed to do just that. Even if that meant protecting her from himself. They both knew from experience what could happen in childbirth and it wasn't going to happen to Ellie because of him.

Lem's eyes narrowed. "Boy, you got more room in that stubborn heart of yours. All you've got to do is open up."

There was more involved than that now, and Mathew knew it. He didn't want anything to happen to Ellie. He couldn't stand to think of it.

"Look-a-there," Lem hooted, spotting a calf caught in a bramble.

Mathew was relieved to have something to distract Lem from the subject at hand. Dismounting, they went to untangle the little fella.

It hit Mathew hard, knowing even his cows had him looking out for them. Caring for them. Ellie hadn't even had that.

The calf bawled as Mathew tore the brambles off of it.

Looking into the young calf's big brown eyes, Mathew's stomach felt ill thinking of Ellie as a child. "Everyone should have someone looking out for them," he said more to himself than to Lem. He lifted his gaze to his friend, who held the animal still. "This calf has us. Ellie deserved someone looking out for her—"

"She's got you," Lem said, puzzlement in his eyes.

"Yeah, and she'd look me square in the face and tell me God was looking out for her. But God wasn't looking out for Beth."

Lem looked sorrowful. "Son, you got to let that go. God's got mysterious ways. Everyone is appointed a time to die when they are still in the womb. That ain't got nothin' to do with you."

Mathew tore away the stickered vines. "God forsook Beth, sweet Beth. And left her baby motherless." Left him with a gaping hole in his heart out here in the middle of the wilderness where they'd planned to build a life together.

Ellie's face, so brave in the face of everything he'd seen thrown her way, blurred his vision. He pulled the calf free and pulled it into his arms.

"Let it go, I'm tellin' you. Quit thinking about what you ain't got and think about what you have."

"Lem, it's not that easy. Look, I'm gonna head on home. We'll see y'all at the party. Ellie is so excited about it."

"Maybe you should do some prayin' on the ride home."

Instead of responding, Mathew hoisted the calf in front of the saddle, then he climbed up behind it. "Tell Maggie thanks, we'll see you there in a few hours," he said as he tugged on the reins, turning his horse around and urging him to a quick pace. It was time to get home.

* * *

The sun was hanging low on the horizon as they headed toward Lem and Maggie's late that afternoon. "Do you think there will be a lot of people there," Ellie asked, barely able to contain her excitement.

"Probably all of Madison, Brazos and Leon County."

"Really?" Ellie gasped, bouncing Sophie on her lap as the buckboard rolled along the bumpy road. Mathew chuckled, sliding his warm gaze her way, teasing her. That look sent her heart fluttering. She'd learned to control her temper somewhat and take her time where Mathew was concerned.

No, she was relying on God to help her not overwhelm Mathew.

She'd first wondered about why a man like him would need to send off for a mail-order bride. Well, no maybes about it, he absolutely had a broken heart.

He'd loved Beth as Ellie could only dream of being loved. He'd said he couldn't give his heart to Ellie, and now she understood. When you loved someone like that…how could you ever risk opening up like that again. Or even have any love left to give after having felt so deeply.

No, Ellie could only pray that she could show Mathew the depth of her own love for him and that at some point he might be able to share enough affection toward her that their marriage could become one of contentment. Maybe she could love him enough for both of them.

"I can't believe they are having a party for *us*," she said. Imagining the evening ahead, she smiled happily at Mathew. He chuckled. The husky sound of it and the sparkle in his eyes had her breathless and thinking of nothing but the moment.

"You deserve it," he said, touching her hand and sending her heart into a gallop.

"Paudy fo us," Sophie said, looking expectantly from Ellie to Mathew. She'd begun forming short sentences within the last few days and sometimes they were understandable. Ellie laughed in delight.

"Yes indeed. Baby girl. A paudy for us."

There were buggies and wagons all over the place as they drove into the yard. Maggie had set up the party in the barn and the doors were flung open wide to let the breeze in. Mathew took Sophie and then helped Ellie from the wagon. She smoothed the skirt of the yellow calico dress with the simple lace collar. Her excitement overshadowed any and all nerves.

"You look lovely this evening, Ellie" Mathew said.

Ellie's gaze swung to him—she wasn't quite sure how to respond to his compliment. *A thank you would be a nice start.* His eyes were warm with appreciation. Ellie heaved in a very unladylike breath. "Thank you. I…I removed some of the ruffles and that awful thick petticoat—" She clamped her mouth shut, not comfortable discussing undergarments with him. Even if he was her husband.

His rich chuckle rumbled deep in his chest. "It suits you much better this way." He held out his arm. "May I have the pleasure, ma'am."

Ellie took his arm, and they walked together toward the festivities.

"Look who is here," Maggie exclaimed as they stepped inside the large barn.

Ellie was so happy to see her new friend and hugged her hard. "This is so wonderful. You've gone to so much trouble, though. You shouldn't have."

"I ain't done nothin' I wasn't happy to do. Now

come on in here and meet your neighbors. And tell me how this handsome cowboy of yours is treating you." She winked at Mathew as she took Sophie from him. Mathew shook his head and grinned.

"Well, lands sakes! That's a smile if I ever saw one, and I didn't have to draw it out of you like thick molasses." She looked at Ellie and beamed. "You done good, girl. Real good. Now come on, you two. We got folks to meet and mingle with, and then there's gonna be hors of dancing. Lem—Lem!" she yelled, motioning to Lem, who was deep in conversation with several other men. "Get yorself over here and greet Ellie."

Ellie spent a delightful hour meeting people who were just happy to meet her. There were several younger women, new brides themselves, who lived out on surrounding ranches like she did. Though there was distance between them, it was nice knowing she had females she could hopefully one day call friends rather than neighbors.

Soon the music began to play. Cute little man that Lem was, with his barrel chest and short legs, played a fierce fiddle. Ellie found herself standing beside the punch bowl tapping her toes to the music. Mathew had been hovering close to her side for most of the first hour, even putting his hand on the small of her back as she was being introduced around. Ellie couldn't help but feel proud that this handsome man was hers and that he seemed more than pleased to call her his.

When she and a group of younger ladies began comparing the progression of their babies, Mathew excused himself and headed over to talk with the men.

She'd watched as he'd approached and the others slapped him on the back in what appeared to be congratulations, so many times that she was certain he would have a bruises by morning.

When the music started Mary, Elizabeth and Rebecca had all hurried to pull their husbands onto the dance floor. Ellie eased to the side of the refreshment table, out of the way as she sipped her punch and watched, memorizing the steps as couples twirled around the center of the barn. Dancing had always looked so fun.

Mathew was deep in conversation with two men outside beside the front doors. Ellie wondered what they were talking about. Sophie played over in the corner with several of the other babies as a group of older women and young girls watched over them. Maggie had insisted that Ellie have a good time and not worry about Sophie. She was in good hands.

"You should be dancing," Mathew said, coming up behind her, leaning close to her ear.

Ellie's heart jumped inside her chest. "No." She was so happy he was here to stand beside her. "I don't dance. But it's lovely to watch and I love the music. Lem and the band play wonderfully."

She turned her head, looking over her shoulder at Mathew. He remained behind her, bent slightly, staring into her eyes. His warm breath on her skin sent a shiver through her.

"You don't dance? You didn't tell me that. I'm not much of a dancer myself, but I'd take you for a spin if you'd like."

She looked at the floor then met his eyes. "No,

that's alright. Watching is fine."

Questions and skepticism in his eyes, Mathew moved beside her as he glanced at the dance floor, then back at her. "Every young girl I know loves to dance, Ellie."

She couldn't meet his gaze but gave a quick smile, willing him to just let this go so they could enjoy the rest of the evening.

Unexpectedly, Mathew took her chin between his fingers and lifted her face so she was forced to look him in the eyes. "What's going on, Ellie?"

How could the man read her so well?

"Oh fiddle, Mathew. I, don't know how to dance, if you must know." There she'd admitted it. His mouth fell open ever so slightly before he clamped it shut.

"Everyone knows how to dance," he said, after a heartbeat.

She shook her head as the music slid straight into a second song.

"Why don't you know how to dance? Don't tell me, dear old Aunt Millicent never took you to a dance." Matthew's face was incredulous.

It almost made Ellie smile. "I went to only a few dances. But, honestly, Mathew this isn't important."

"No, Ellie," he said gently. "It is important. Why don't you know how to dance?"

Ellie huffed. "Well, if you must know. I was never *asked* to dance." There, she'd admitted that too..

CHAPTER ELEVEN

Mathew could not believe his ears. Ellie a *wallflower*. Frustration at the injustice of it all engulfed him like a Texas grass fire. "Your part of Fort Worth was full of a of fools." He stepped in front of Ellie, hating the sting of humiliation in her eyes. He'd come to know Ellie as the most vibrant and alive person he'd ever met. She played with Sophie with the abandon of a child herself and she looked at the work on the ranch as an adventure.

Tamping down his anger, he pulled Ellie into his arms. "May I have this dance, Mrs. McConnell?"

Her eyes flew wide in shock. "No." She shook her head and pushed against his arms.

"What?" Baffled, Mathew held on. "Ellie. Dance

with me."

"Mathew, no. I...I can't," she hissed softly. "I've never danced before. I don't know what to *do*."

He smiled, glad that he was about to be the one to dance with her first. "Take my hand, Ellie. Trust me." He held her worried eyes with his, willing her to trust him. She breathed in deeply, her lips grim as she looked from his offered hand to his eyes. He smiled. "You're not scared are you?"

Her blue eyes fired up and her jaw jutted out. *There's some spirit,* he thought, knowing the barb would bring back that fire back that he'd come to love. She jammed her fingers into his hand, hiked her chin and held his gaze. He pulled her closer and his heart kicked like a bull

Despite trying not to, had he fallen in love with Ellie? Somehow that thought wasn't as troubling as it had been in the not-too-distant past.

"You lead," she ground out. "I'll follow."

He grinned, touched his forehead to hers, processing his emotions. "I like the sound of that, Ellie." Fighting the urge to kiss her, he warned instead. "Hang on, honey and go with me." And then he spun her out onto the dance floor, practically lifting her up as he went.

Tonight, his wife was going to dance like nobody had ever danced before.

* * *

The stars were shinning as they waved their good-byes. Ellie glanced into the bed of the wagon where Sophie was snuggled, fast asleep on the soft blankets Mathew had laid out for her. "Sophie had a wonderful evening," Ellie said, as Mathew turned the horses onto the road and headed toward home.

"How about you, Ellie? Did you have a good time?"

Mathew's gentle question wrapped around her like a warm blanket and Ellie could not help but long for his arms once more. "I had a *glorious* time." Her gaze locked with his and a shiver raced through her.

"Good," he said, grinning. "You are a fast learner."

"I had a great teacher. I'm thinking you must have

never missed a dance growing up." The man had danced with her until she thought her feet would fall off and then they'd danced some more. She hadn't wanted to stop. Stopping meant his arms wouldn't be around her any longer. Oh, how, she loved this man. How could she not?

"I had my fair share of dances, it's true," he said. Clucking, he urged the team to pick up their pace a bit, then looked back at her. "But no one has ever been more fun to dance with than you."

Ellie's breath caught and her heart stilled. *Oh Mathew, if you could only love me.*

Not knowing what to say, Ellie simply smiled and then looked up at the stars. There were thousands of them tonight.

They traveled in silence. Her heart was overflowing with the beauty of what she and Mathew had shared tonight. She didn't want to spoil any of it by asking...by pushing for more.

She wouldn't be greedy. She must be content.

They'd turned off the road and were crossing their land now, the lane illuminated by the soft moonlight and the canopy of brilliant stars.

"Did Beth love to dance?" Ellie asked at long last. The question burst from her in the silence and it was between them before she could stop it. She was hopeless!

Mathew sat up straighter and she wasn't sure he was going to answer. "Yes, she did," he said at last. Then, meeting her gaze, he added, "Almost as much as you."

Pressing her lips together, she held back the smile that yearned to bloom at his words. "Do you miss her terrible?" she asked softly, feeling for him.

He nodded. "I think I always will."

He sounded so wistful, it was just as she'd thought. Heart clutching, she closed her eyes and let his words sink in. They had come to this companionable relationship, but that was all it would ever be.

Mathew slowed the buckboard and came to a halt. "Ellie, look at me."

Ellie thought her heart would burst. She couldn't look at him. How, oh how, could she be jealous of a dead woman?

Forcing herself to have some dignity she looked at him and smiled. "She was a very lucky woman."

He'd stopped the buckboard just before a bend in the road and there was a stand of trees. "Ellie, listen to me." He took her in his arms. "I am a lucky man. A blessed man," he said. He was lowering his lips to hers when suddenly three cows rounded the bend in the road, flanked by two riders.

Mathew let go of Ellie, pushed her behind him protectively as he reached for his gun.

"I wouldn't do that if I were you," said the man who approached on their right, the click of his rifle's hammer sounding as he aimed it straight at Ellie. It gleamed ominously in the moonlight.

Mathew went stone still beside her. "Don't move, Ellie. Don't speak. Just go easy."

To them he said. "Don't do anything you'll regret in the morning." One man had a beard, its shadow visible in the light, though his hat shadowed the rest of his face. The taller one with the gun wore a duster and she couldn't his facial features beneath his hat either.

"I'm thinkin' we ain't got much choice in the

matter. Seein as how you know these are your cattle."

Ellie couldn't move. Stealing cattle was a hanging offense. So what would they have to lose if they hurt them in the process? Or worse?

"Why don't you toss that six-shooter you're holding this direction. Or I use the little lady for target practice."

Ellie gasped. "Mathew—"

"Hush, Ellie. Just hold tight." Mathew tossed his weapon to the ground.

They were now at these varmints. Ellie glanced over her shoulder at Sophie. Sweet Sophie. She would do what she needed to do to try and save her baby.

The bearded rider walked his horse over and looked down at them. "Boss, they've got a baby over here."

"That so."

"Yeah, I don't know about no baby."

"Get out of the wagon, you two," the boss guy demanded, ignoring his partner. "And bring that baby with you."

Ellie could hardly breathe. She prayed that God would help them. Prayed that Mathew wouldn't do anything careless. Maybe if they just did as they were told they'd be spared.

She reached for Sophie. Mathew started to help her but the man with the beard leveled his rifle on him. "You stay still."

Ellie pulled Sophie into her arms as gently as she could, but the child woke up and immediately began to wail.

"Get that cryin' baby to shutup," the boss ordered. "And get down off that wagon."

Mathew nodded and Ellie eased out of the wagon clutching Sophie to her. Once they were on the ground, she tried to soothe Sophie, but she could not be consoled. Maybe it was waking up in the dark in a strange place that had her disturbed. Or seeing these strange faces. Ellie clung to her and prayed for God to intervene.

"Now you get out of the wagon," the bearded man commanded. Mathew took his time, never taking his eyes off the man. A dangerous look in Mathew's eyes, set alarms off inside Ellie. What was he thinking about doing?

"You know they have descriptions of you," he said, moving to stand at the head of the wagon. "I talked with the sheriff this evening and he said he got the Wanted posters today. Your time in this area is numbered."

"What we gonna do with these three? Leave 'em, they can't do nothin' to us," the bearded outlaw asked. "We need to get out of Texas. Fast."

"Take them into the woods and get rid of them. Now git," the boss man spat out. "And quit your bellyaching."

Mathew had placed himself between the two riders, and Ellie was pretty certain he'd done it for a reason. Part of that reason was to distance them from her and Sophie, who were still standing on the other side of the wagon. Sophie was still carrying on. Ellie was so distraught she was sure the baby could sense it.

An owl hooted from the woods and Ellie shivered. Would this be the end of them?

"Why don't you two think this through," Mathew said calmly. "If you start now, you'll be well on your way out of this county by morning. We'll keep our mouths shut and give you time to make it out. Just let my wife and baby go. Killing a woman and child is going to bring a rain of fire down on you. You'll be hunted down—"

The boss galloped his horse over to Mathew and poked his pistol at Mathew's chest. "Keep your mouth shut," he snapped.

"But, boss, he's got a point. If we kill them, we'll never have any peace."

To Ellie's dismay, the boss leveled his gun on his partner. "Climb down off that horse and do as I've told you or I'll shoot you myself. Do you hear?"

Muttering, the man did as he was told. Grumbling, he poked Mathew in the back and shoved him with his gun. "You heard the man. Git!"

Mathew's jaw tightened but he said nothing as he met Ellie's gaze over the wagon. Ellie was rocking Sophie, trying desperately to quite her cries, and she realized Mathew was not going to go down without a fight. He was not going to just let these men walk them into the woods and shoot them. He would die trying to save them.

Oh, Lord. "Please, listen to him," Ellie blurted over

Sophie's wails. "You've just stolen some cattle. You don't want to do this."

"Ellie, quite now," Mathew demanded. "Stay right where you are."

"Hey," the boss growled. "I'm giving the orders here and I'm telling the little lady to make nice and get over here with you."

Mathew had a rifle jammed in his back. He was only about three steps from the rustler on the horse, that man's gun now pointed straight at Ellie. Tension was so high, electricity vibrated in the air. Ellie didn't move, couldn't move—it was as if God had put a hand on her shoulder and was holding her in place just as a low, thunderous rumble sounded through the trees.

Thunder? Sophie's tears had soaked her shirt, and Ellie clutched the dear child closer to her heart and bent her lips to her sweaty hair. "Please, please calm down little darlin'" she whispered but she wailed louder and the thunder drew closer—Ellie recognized the sound just as Prudence burst from the trees charging straight forward.

Chaos erupted!

The two horses hitched to the wagon bolted and broke for home, startling the outlaws. Mathew grabbed the riffle from the man on the ground and wrenched it from his hands just as Prudence hit the man full force and plowed right over him. The boss man was trying to control his horse as Mathew dove for him, grabbed him, and yanked him from the rearing horse. The outlaw hit the ground with a thud. A gun went off, and Ellie realized she was standing in the open with Sophie in her arms!

"Dear Lord, keep Mathew safe," she yelled and ran for the trees. Shots ringing out behind her. She planted her back to the first oak she came to. Sophie had stopped crying and in the shadowed darkness Ellie could see the whites of her eyes; they were as round as saucers. Feeling the little girl's limbs and torso, Ellie satisfied herself that none of the gunshots had hit her. Breathing heavily, Ellie prayed hard, then turned, keeping Sophie as close to the trunk as she dared to peek around the edge.

To her relief, Mathew had the gun and had it aimed at the outlaw whose arms were in the air. The second outlaw wasn't doing as well; he was flat on his stomach with Prudence sitting on top of him.

It was over.

"*Ellie*," Mathew yelled. "Are you and Sophie alright?"

Ellie almost cried at the fear and concern she heard in his voice. "Yes," she called, feeling weaker than she ever had. He was safe.

They were safe.

God had seen them through.

And Prudy did own this ranch now and could sleep inside by the fire this winter if she wanted too. Anything. Anything at all that mule wanted, that mule could have!

CHAPTER TWELVE

At dawn's light, Ellie had strong coffee brewing. She stood by the window, waiting. Mathew had tied the two outlaws together and lashed them to a tree. Then he pulled a saddle from one of the outlaw's horses and placed it on Prudence. Once that was done he held Sophie while Ellie climbed into the saddle. He put Sophie in front of Ellie and let Prudence bring them home.

He went for the sheriff.

Ellie had rocked her sleeping Sophie for the next four hours and waited. Finally she'd placed her baby into her bed, closed the door and made coffee. Then she'd made biscuits. And now she waited some more. Before long she'd make something else just to keep her hands busy.

Where is he?

So much had happened since the first time she'd scanned Wishing Springs and asked that same question.

Her life was so much richer than it had been then. Things weren't as she'd dreamed, but she could live with that. If only he'd come home and she could see his face.

He'd said he missed Beth. She'd heard the love and regret in his voice. Closing her eyes, she accepted the blessings that she had gained and tried not to long for what lay behind the doors God had closed.

Hoofbeats. She looked out the front door and saw him coming.

So strong and powerful in the saddle. Hurrying outside, still in her dress from the party, she didn't care if she fell down. She raced across the yard, skirts flapping and tangling as she ran. At the edge of the corral she stopped, put her hand to her forehead, and watched him gallop her way. The man was born to ride.

Jumping from the saddle, he didn't stop until he had her in his arms.

Ellie buried her face in his chest, her hands gripping his shirt. She breathed in the very essence of him. *Thank You, Lord, for bringing him home.* "You're safe," she sobbed.

"It's alright, Ellie. It's over." He ran his hands down her back and over her arms and then he hugged her tight and his lips brushed the skin of her neck. Ellie went still in his arms. Letting herself savor the moment.

"I thought I was going to lose you, Ellie," he said, his voice broke.

Had he said what she thought he said?

He lifted his head, and took her face in his hands. "Ellie, I love you. I've been trying to deny it. But I was a fool."

Warmth and light exploded inside Ellie at his words. Her heart was bursting and she couldn't contain the smile that took over her face. But did she dare believe—"Oh Mathew. I thought, when you told me you would always miss Beth that there was never any hope for me."

He sobered. "I will always miss Beth. She is part of me, and always will be. But you are too, Ellie. You are my blessing from God. I have been too blind to realize it. I feel so humbled that God would send me you—" He stopped speaking and his brows dipped into that scowl that she'd come to love. "Wait, you haven't said—"

"I *love* you, Mathew," Ellie said with emotion, then pressed her lips to his. "I've loved you from the first moment I read the ad—"

Before she could say anything more, Mathew covered her mouth with his, kissing her with all the love and longing she'd dreamed of. Skin-tingling, toe-curling, heart- pounding love poured into her and left her breathless. There was the promise of a future and a family in that kiss, and Ellie's knees would have given out beneath her if Mathew hadn't been crushing her so tightly in his arms.

Suddenly he broke the kiss and pulled back to look at her. "Wait, I didn't write the lovely words you fell for."

She laughed as joy filling her soul. "The promise of you and Sophie were in those words. They gave me courage to change my life and a hope that I could have a future with you. And I loved the idea of you. And knowing you, being with you each day, has only made my love stronger."

"I love you, Ellie McConnell. And I want to spend the rest of my days showing you just how much."

"Now that is what I love about you, Mathew. You are a man of your word." Ellie smiled and took his hand. "I think it's time you moved into the house."

Mathew threw back his head and laughed, a deep rumbling laugh that filled Ellie with more happiness. What a life they would have. "Lead on, Ellie. Let's get started."

Ellie winked at him. "I couldn't agree more," she said, and together they walked toward their home, their baby and a future that promised to be richer and fuller than any fairy tale or happy ending Ellie could have dreamed of. God was so good.

They walked to the house and Ellie hugged Prudence once more—she had been standing at the front porch like a sentinel since bringing them safely home.

"Thank you, Prudy. You saved us." Ellie kissed the old mule's forehead. Prudy had heard Sophie's wails and come searching for her baby, and rescued them.

"Hey," Mathew said, "*I* rescued you and Sophie."

"Now, Mathew don't be jealous. You know perfectly well that Prudy galloped in and saved the day."

"She might have started it but I finished it."

"Why, Mathew, surely you aren't jealous of a little ole mule," Ellie teased, unable to help herself.

"Well of course not." Mathew opened the door and scowled.

"That's good. Because I have a special place in my heart—" Ellie's teasing was cut short when he swept her into his arms and covered her lips with his.

And then he carried her over the threshold and kicked the door closed behind him.

Ellie met his kiss with her heart. They were home…

And Prudy was on guard.

About the Author

Debra Clopton is a USA Today bestselling & International bestselling author who has sold over 3.5 million books. She has published over 81 books under her name and her pen name of Hope Moore.

Under both names she writes clean & wholesome and inspirational, small town romances, especially with cowboys but also loves to sweep readers away with romances set on beautiful beaches surrounded by topaz water and romantic sunsets.

Her books now sell worldwide and are regulars on the Bestseller list in the United States and around the world. Debra is a multiple award-winning author, but of all her awards, it is her reader's praise she values most. If she can make someone smile and forget their worries for a few hours (or days when binge reading one of her series) then she's done her job and her heart is happy. She really loves hearing she kept a reader from doing the dishes or sleeping!

A sixth-generation Texan, Debra lives on a ranch in Texas with her husband surrounded by cattle, deer, very busy squirrels and hole digging wild hogs. She enjoys traveling and spending time with her family.

Visit Debra's website and sign up for her newsletter for updates at: www.debraclopton.com

Check out her Facebook at:
www.facebook.com/debra.clopton.5

Follow her on Instagram at: debraclopton_author

or contact her at debraclopton@ymail.com

www.ingramcontent.com/pod-product-compliance
Lightning Source LLC
LaVergne TN
LVHW011839060526
838200LV00054B/4108